Bibi Ukonu

THINGS THAT START
SMALL
BUT SWEET

THINGS THAT START

SMALL

BUT SWEET

Griots Lounge Publishers Canada

Email: hello@griotslounge.com

ISBN 978-1-7772756-0-0
First published in English Language by Griots Lounge Publishers 2017

Printed in Canada

For **Georgina,** *faith and courage personified.*

ACKNOWLEDGEMENTS

In early 2016, I had already given up as a creative writer. I had made up my mind to birth a magazine that focused more on architecture and sustainable urban development. And this meant getting my hands involved in a lot of social works with non-governmental organizations in and out of Nigeria, writing about the poor housing conditions of the urban poor, appreciating their resilience against all negative odds, and using architecture and smart technology to find solutions to the many challenges faced by these dwellers. While working with Justice and Empowerment Initiatives, an NGO based in Lagos and Port Harcourt that advocates for the urban poor dwellers of waterfront communities, I found a waterfront fishing community by the coastal lines the megacity of Lagos—Makoko. I fell in love.

I specially thank the people of Makoko Community, and also the demolished settlement of Otodo-Gbame, for bringing me back to write this collection of short stories. This collection is yours. To Justina Edukpo and Mathew Kusika, I am deeply grateful for trusting me and teaching me the ways of the beautiful Egun people. To Megan Chapman and Andrew Maki of Justice and Empowerment Initiatives, I will always echo your bellows concerning social inclusion. And to Tatiana Alecia Smith of PHIDAS Washington, thanks for trusting a stranger.

And these guys here are my A+ people: Omoregie Osakpolor—for all the lovely images of beautiful people and following me to Makoko all the time; EC Osondu for the encouragements; Onyeka Nwelue for being there; Ben Preye Baldwin for being a brother and a beautiful soul; and to Charles Okereke, Linus Okorie, Bura Bari Nwilo, Mitterand Okorie, Chika Unigwe, Uche Peter Umez, Chigozie Ofor, David Ishaya Osu, and my entire Facebook family. I also appreciate my VVIP, 'Tayo Keyede, my editor, and Jideofor Aluka, my publisher.

My love for my dad and siblings is immeasurable. You are my first fans. To Ada, Chisimdi, Muna, and Harida, thanks for tolerating a writer in the house, and all those days you let me be by myself, just to check me up at intervals to ask if I was done, or if I needed to snack on something. I love you.

These are stories that stay with you long after you finish reading them. Ukonu is a writer with something to say–pay attention.

–E.C. OSONDU
Winner The Caine Prize

Ukonu's characters have been empowered to live and inspire, and not become pitied. Though the backdrop, where they are coming from is messy, their lives are amusing and quite fascinating. And sometimes you see choice, the decision to walk away from perceived discomfort.

–BURA-BARI NWILO,
Author of *A Tiny Place Called Happiness*

Bibi Ukonu's work grapples with all that we are and see around us, portraying the beauty in things we sometimes overlook, while highlighting the tragedy of class and power within the Nigerian society. These are fantastic stories told with a calm and gentle voice.

–MITTERAND OKORIE
Author of *All That Was Bright and Ugly*

Lyrical, nuanced and flowing beautifully, Bibi Ukonu is Nigeria's finest short story writer.

–ONYEKA NWELUE
Author of *The Abyssinian Boy*

Said hands to the rest,
"I feed you all to fat,"
Said legs to the rest,
"I take you to the food."

Said the mouth to all,
"I make them know you're here"
Said eyes to them all,
"I see before you talk."

Said nose to the rest,
"I smell good soup up there,"
Said ears to the rest,
"I hear spoons clanking plates."

"I take you to the top,"
Said brain to them all,
Said heart to the brain,
"Speak not, or I will stop."

Speak Not–Bibi Ukonu (2009)

THINGS THAT PROSPER US

At Akanja's shrine, Ndukamkpa made known the plans he had been harboring a few years after he lost his job at the brewery in Awo. He had just nailed corrugated roofing sheets as a covering for a few timber columns he had collected from construction sites that had no more need for them. And because he believed he was God-sent, he visited Akanja that early Saturday morning, before those who slept at night could stretch their bones before the orange-colored lights of the morning. He said many things to Akanja and he dropped three tubers of Igbo yam and one cockerel.

Akanja smiled as Ndukamkpa dropped the gifts close to the burning incense on the bare red mud that finished the floor. Akanja was not new to his wishes, as many men of God had visited his shrine requesting powers to perform all sorts of weird and unbelievable phenomena, even the ones Akanja found hilarious. And Akanja, the renowned voodooist and conjurer, would always ask them out of his shrine because he believed one needed to be loyal to his god. But that morning, as Ndukamkpa walked into the shrine and made known his desire to grow his new church, Akanja cringed and obliged him the comfort of his wooden stool.

After Akanja had given him a blue handkerchief and told him to wipe his face with it three times before starting up any church day, he broke kola and offered Ndukamkpa one part of the four parts. Ndukamkpa accepted his kola and snacked

1

immediately. He was to wipe his face only three times with the blue handkerchief and to use the yellow face towel to clean any sweat afterward. It was the only way he could get his congregation to believe his every word and instructions, and also get them to win more souls for him.

Ndukamkpa did not spend much time with Akanja that morning. He stood and left the shrine as soon as the witch doctor was done with his incantations. Ndukamkpa left the shrine with his shoulders squared and a smile that drew both ends of his lips close to his ears. He walked briskly down the bush path and onto the express lane, where he found a taxi driving along and down the road to his low-income housing where he lived with his wife and three daughters.

On Sunday morning, after Ndukamkpa had obeyed the instructions of Akanja and wiped his face three times with the blue handkerchief, he sat down close to the altar and sang and prayed, and spent that whole morning alone, without a single individual as his congregation. Even Uloma, his wife, did not believe in Ndukamkpa's new calling. She insisted that she would remain a staunch member of the local Anglican Church in Amakohia, where they lived. That morning, while Ndukamkpa woke early to make it to his *Cries of the Cross Church International*, Uloma dressed her daughters up, gave them their Bibles and hymn books, and led them out of the house because she insisted that they were never to miss the Sunday School classes which were just before the main service in the Anglican Church. Uloma would tell Ndukamkpa that God would one day clean the deceit that clogged his thinking, and would return him to the Anglican Church. Ndukamkpa would laugh and say something about

Uloma's ignorance of God and his spiritual calling.

"A prophet is not known in his town," he would tell his wife and shake his head in disapproval.

After that lonely Sunday, Ndukamkpa strategized and hatched a plan. On his way home, he went to the roadside kiosk where Hassan and Adamu, the Hausas from the north, sold petty goods and repaired bad shoes. Ndukamkpa pleaded with them to attend next Sunday's service. While he spoke, Ndukamkpa continued wiping his face with the blue handkerchief, over and over. He knew he needed to make them a promise to win their hearts. So he asked Hassan to supply the church with sweets every Sunday, and Adamu was to polish his shoes to make him look good. And then he promised them little refreshment immediately after each Sunday service. Hassan and Adamu agreed to his offers, in excitement, clapping their hands and giggling.

"*Insha Allah*, we go come church next Sunday bah," Hassan said. "We will come, Oga. Don't worry."

"God bless you two," Ndukamkpa prayed. "May His light shine upon you."

"Amiiin," chorused both men.

The following Sunday morning, as Ndukamkpa walked into his church, Hassan and Adamu had already swept dried leaves off the mud floors of the church and were seated and waiting for him. Ndukamkpa, the dark and petite figure, exhaled and emptied the air in his bowel. He smiled, shook hands with his new and only congregation, wiped his face with the blue handkerchief and became possessed by a spirit that made him speak in languages that never had any meaning. He then began to run in a circle, around the corners of his church, around the scanty plastic chairs, and around Hassan and Adamu. He screamed and yelled many words, and prominent was the name of Jehovah Jireh, who he also called the Prince of Peace. But Ndukamkpa's prayer was nothing close to peace. It looked like he had an unfinished battle with principalities and powers in high places. Hassan and Adamu stared at him as he jogged around them, and they chuckled and veiled their mouths with their hands so Ndukamkpa would not hear them laughing. Ndukamkpa did not hear them, but he came to an abrupt stop. He preached the sermon of the day, and Hassan and Adamu did not understand one word that he preached from the Bible.

When Ndukamkpa was satisfied, he offered them malt drinks and some groundnuts, and they ate and drank, and were happy. They were happy because no one had mentioned it before, in Amakohia, that there was a church that refreshed members with cold drinks and nuts after wearing them out with loud and noisy shouts. Hassan and Adamu went back to their shop and told each customer that came that week beautiful things about Ndukamkpa's church, especially that he never asked for offering, yet he fed his congregation. That was how Ndukamkpa became a popular preacher in Amakohia, and Cries of the Cross Church International grew from a congregation of two to a little over two hundred. And Uloma said she knew Ndukamkpa was truly called by God. She joined him with her daughters and became the leader of the women of the church.

A few months after, Ndukamkpa announced that it was time to ask for cash offerings because the Lord needed to grow his church. It was then that Hassan and Adamu stopped attending church services, and Ndukamkpa never noticed they had stopped. Rather, after every service, he would gather in his living room with Uloma and her daughters to count and record the day's proceeds. He also did not bother when Uloma stopped giving members refreshment after service. No one bothered about that, not the church members that kept growing in number. People stopped attending their various churches; the beautiful people of Amakohia – old and young, because Ndukamkpa had begun performing miracles and healing broken limbs and barren wombs. People went to him for prayers and for solutions to many challenges. And for every prayer or counseling, Ndukamkpa made sure the people brought varying amounts of cash which he said would open God's ears to their cries, and he built his church, bought SUV cars, wore designer suits and shoes, and bought and renovated his house from his landlord. Even though Ndukamkpa was a small man, his words and aura stood quite tall in every street, home and corner of Amakohia and neighboring environs.

Ndukamkpa always returned to Akanja, once every month, and the more he visited, the bigger his offerings became. Akanja was obviously happy with Ndukamkpa. He would wear smiles on his face and tell Ndukamkpa private stories about himself. He told him about his childhood and how he ran far away from home because his father insisted on resting the oracle on him. His father and the father before him worshipped Ikonna, the god of good seeds. Ikonna had become the family god and had been handed over from one generation to another. When Akanja heard his father utter his name as next-in-line, he left his father's hut at midnight and ran as fast as the cheetah to the city where began to work as a mechanic.

It was not long before Akanja fell ill and became incurable, and his kind master began to search for his relatives. Six months after Akanja ran away from Amakohia to the city, and everyone cried and searched for him before deciding he was dead and never to return, Akanja was brought back home half-dead by his master. His father took him from the hands of his master, carried him into the hut, mixed some concoctions which Akanja swallowed and slept off. He woke up after an entire week. Akanja woke up quite healthy and has remained in Amakohia, where the oracle of Ikonna was handed over to him by the gods after his father's death.

While munching kola nuts and drinking local gin, Akanja would tell Ndukamkpa many stories of things that had happened to him in the past. And when Ndukamkpa had led his massive congregation for a little over a year, Akanja slept and never woke up. He lay on the floor of his shrine, next to the carved figurine of the oracle and was buried by the government after his corpse decayed and the powerful, pungent and disgusting smell began to infiltrate the neighborhood. Akanja had no wife and children because he wanted to bring the existence of Ikonna to an end. Ikonna died with Akanja. And the stories only existed in Ndukamkpa's memories.

Three years after Ndukamkpa started his church, he had built and roofed it, and it stood as a symbolic landmark in Amakohia. The red roof tiles that covered the massive structure announced the presence of the building from two kilometers away, and many went to admire the walls that were finished with marble and the entire beauty of the worship center. Uloma had also changed. She wore costly dinner gowns to church services, and her concoction of different perfumes easily permeated the air that filled the interior of the church, from one nostril to the other.

The church members had baptized Ndukamkpa and Uloma with new names—*Papa* and *Mama*. And the congregation now grew beyond Amakohia and the city as people drove from far away towns and cities in search of solutions to one problem or the other. Ndukamkpa had touched the forehead of an old woman who instantly claimed she had her sight back after over a decade of blindness. Many women said he cuddled their stomachs and they became fruitful and gave birth to babies. He had done many things which many doubted, while much more believed in the efficacy of his utterances. Ndukamkpa would speak promises into empty plastic bottles, seal them and sell to his congregation.

"This is the air of life," Ndukamkpa would stand before the multitude of worshipers and declare. "Buy and hide under your bed. Wherever the air of life is cannot be polluted."

"Hallelujah!" some would shout.

"Amen!" many more would approve.

Ndukamkpa became so powerful. His words filtered into different homes until he became an authority and the guideline to how many chose to live.

But that last Sunday in August, three years after he chose Hassan and Adamu as his first worshipers, he sat in his office, his jaws resting in his palms, his head quivering like an earthquake ready to happen. Ndukamkpa sweated all over his face, and as the sweat trekked along his chins, it washed away the powder he had applied early that morning. A massive congregation of worshipers was already singing and dancing and waiting for Ndukamkpa to make an appearance in the church hall. Uloma was standing by her husband's side, cuddling his shoulder.

"I have searched for it," Ndukamkpa said, "All over the house. I searched and turned over everything in the bedroom, even the car."

"And you're sure you searched every corner?" Uloma asked. "It never leaves your suitcase. I'm surprised you can't find it in there."

"I'm surprised too. This is just strange," he said. He sat up and moved aside his chair. Uloma moved away from the desk. Ndukamkpa walked around the office, and then stood before his bookshelf where he brought each book out and replaced them as if he had earlier kept something inside the shelf.

"Can't you preach without that handkerchief?" Uloma finally breaks the silence. "The people are waiting for you. The choristers will soon run out of songs to keep them busy."

"I've said it over a million times, Uloma," Ndukamkpa yelled. "That handkerchief is the power of my ministry. It is the mantle. It is the reason I am powerful. I've wanted to say this to you, Uloma."

"Say what to me, Ndu?" Uloma asked.

"That I have not been honest with you. I've not been honest with God and the people," he continued. "I am evil. This is not God's power. God is not using me."

"Calm down, Ndu," Uloma said. She walked to the shelf and held Ndukamkpa's both hands. She felt the warmth in his hands and the fears that ooze from his eyes.

"What are you saying?" she quivered.

8

"Uloma, the blue handkerchief is Akanja's gift to me," Ndukamkpa said. "The miracles are from Akanja, not me; and definitely not from Jehovah. Akanja is the reason why the people love me. Without the handkerchief, I am ruined. Without the handkerchief, I have no powers. And the people will never listen to me. I have been trying to tell you, Uloma. I am evil."

Uloma slumped into the leather settee, close to the bookshelf, tears rushing down her cheeks, she threw one pillow to the desk, and two wooden plaques fell to the tiled floor and shattered into parts. Ndukamkpa did not turn to look. He kept taking out the books from the shelf, and he then started throwing them to the floor. The choir was singing in the church hall, and the congregation was dancing and singing along. Outside, within the church premises, a few volunteers were pointing drivers to where they could park their vehicles as the church lots were all used up. Ndukamkpa peeped through the window and saw the church volunteers. He recognized them from their faces and the reflective jackets he had agreed they would wear. He inhaled air and gasped yet again. He speedily drew the curtain and briskly walked out of the office into the lobby.

Some poles away from the church, Adamu was sweating and getting his polishes and brushes organized. A long line of men and women, with different requests, were before him. Most wanted their shoes polished, while a few needed Adamu to repair their shoes. There was another group that wanted him to quickly open new holes in their leather belts. And there was another group that only came to watch and praise him for how he added a professional touch to his work. Hassan, who also had a lot to sell because Adamu's customers needed to buy a few things, quickly sold and assisted Adamu who had started sweating profusely and quite uneasy with sitting down a long time. The patronage, that morning, did not make the day look like it was a Sunday, and both men were glad and happy that Allah had blessed the day. The more Adamu tried to close out on the demand before him, the more men and women gathered like bees and brought more shoes to him to polish or repair. Hassan took over the polishing of shoes, while Adamu did what he knew best to do, which was to repair shoes that had gone bad. And when he sweated so much that it clogged his eyes and stung, he brought out the blue handkerchief that he had picked close to Ndukamkpa's SUV, and wiped the wetness off his face.

He continued to work.

THINGS THAT START SMALL BUT SWEET

J esufon said he missed the smelly waters of Makoko. He said
that was why he ran away from his master's house. He said
many things that suggested that his master's wife was a real
beast. The day Iya Ahisi took him to Lekki to go and live with the
rich people, his master's wife did not allow him with his tattered
slippers into her living room. He held the slippers in an embrace
while the bleached lady, who spoke quite good English, gave out
her rules and regulations (*her dos and don'ts*) to Iya Ahisi. Of all the
rules and regulations she read out, Jesufon took seriously that she
said he needed to be tested for the different diseases that came
with being poor. Jesufon was to test for malaria and hepatitis and
very many other diseases because she didn't want her children to
contract diseases from a "Makoko" boy. Jesufon was to not to
touch her children until all the tests returned negative. Iya Ahisi
nodded, showed Jesufon where he was to keep his nylon bag of
clothes, and dragged him out of the house afterward.

They arrived at a chemist's where Jesufon"s blood was
sucked with a syringe by a female nurse whom he said looked
quite skinny and pale like she did not live among the rich. Jesufon
did not have any of those diseases he was tested for. But he ran
away from his new master's house the next morning. And it was
not long before we sighted him sailing into the uneven and water
streets of Makoko on a *tojihun*, just like every other Makoko child
that missed home.

"Lagos is not natural," Jesufon says to me as we fetch water from the good water tank into our cans. "They all feel they are superhumans. They don't speak French. And they don't play."

"Iya Ahisi came to see Anonye yesterday," I finally open up to Jesufon. Iya Ahisi is an old lady in her fifties who has no husband and child of her own. She has become known for visiting the very many families in Makoko with huge promises of how big and wealthy Lagos people are; and how she has the connections to transform poor families in Makoko by taking their children to the rich people. Everyone believes Iya Ahisi because she has five *dadihun*, which are bigger than the *tojihun*, and paddle passengers and visitors in and out of Makoko waters. She also brought the white people who cook jollof rice for the kids on weekends and play loud *fuji* music for us to dance and party.

There are also the chubby and cheerful nurses who wear immaculate white gowns, and who come to check on pregnant women to give them drugs and vaccines. It was Iya Ahisi who brought the French teacher from Badagry. He was a tall and dark man with bold eyeballs. He urged me to practice more because he felt I spoke very good French and would one day work for the embassies.

"Why was she at your house to see your mother?" Jesufon asks. He stands up from the bench of his wooden *tojihun* while the canoe rocks from left to right and he gradually finds his balance.

"She should not let Iya Ahisi take Zinwhe away. She is too young for the craziness of the rich people in Lagos. They will take away her innocence and turn her into an adult. She cannot play with their children because she is poor. Don't let your mother give Zinwhe away, Zannu. Don't oh!"

"But Anonye thinks I am too young to tell her what to do," I say to him. "Since Papa was shot by the police for trying to stop them from demolishing Otodo-Gbame, Anonye keeps insisting that she is the only one to say what is to happen in the house."

"She must not allow Iya Ahisi take Zinwhe away," Jesufon insists. His water cans are all filled now. He dips his long bamboo stick into the water and pushes away from the tap head of the storage tank.

"I will paddle to your house in the evening. You'll tell me why she came. Remember, don't allow her to take away your little sister, no matter what."

And he sails away, out of tanks. His canoe clashes with a couple of other *tojihun*. They all rock. Jesufon holds firm to the bamboo stick in his hands and finds balance before pushing on ahead. I hold on to the wooden base of the water tanks and drag my canoe to the tap heads. It is my turn, after Jesufon, to fill up my four yellow cans with water.

In the very early hours of the morning, I run out of Makoko, through Sabo Yaba, with Jesufon and Zinwhe. We run freely; Lagos busy with people who care less about passersby. We run past the *agberos* and the bus conductors bellowing at people on their way to work, market and schools. We run past newspaper vendors untying their bundles of publications. There are a lot of vendors of many fast moving goods on the streets. They all yell at the top of their voices.

Okpa!

Ekor!

Agege bread!

Hot puff-puff!

Hell is real! Give your life to Jesus!

In Makoko, everyone now goes to church. Many families stopped fishing on Sundays. And the beautiful smell of smoked fish, which permeates the air of Makoko, reduces each Sunday in the recent months. Everyone attends the Reformed People Christian Church where Ade is the Pastor-in-charge. But Jesufon and I have not gone to Ade's church.

"Ole!" Jesufon would yell each time Ade's name is mentioned, even worse when people refer to him as *Pastor Ade*. Ade is the *bad boy* of Makoko who leaves at night and returns in the morning with wads of naira notes which he claims was his reward for working for his rich master. Ade is the one who takes all the young boys to the bar and buys them whiskey, rum, and cigarettes. Ade is the very tall and dark boy with no tribal marks, the one the girls always fight to be around. He is the one who impregnated Fifame, Mawuklo, and Hunsi, and fathered very many babies in Makoko. He is the one who returned one morning with blood-stained white shirt. And soon, the story filtered into the smoked fish aroma air of Makoko of how he escaped jungle justice after a robbery attempt in Oshodi. Few months after he was almost burnt alive, he raised a wooden structure by the waterfront and started gathering a congregation of Jesus worshippers.

"Let us run faster!" Jesufon yells. He is already far ahead while Zinwhe is catching up with him. I am losing breath. We had nothing to eat before sneaking out of Makoko in my boat. Jesufon says it is the best time to leave Anonyo and her stubbornness. It is the best time to leave before Iya Ahisi climbs out of her canoe and into our house to come and take me and Zinwhe to the open city where she said she knows some rich Lagos women we will work for, go to school and make better money to support our widowed mother.

"*Ketu-Ojota! Ketu-Ojota!*" yells a young boy who hung by the door of a yellow bus. We run towards him, throwing our weak limbs forward, one after the other. He alights and grabs Jesufon by the hand. Jesufon is forced to a sudden halt while Zinwhe runs into him, trying so hard not to clash. They both fell to the ground as soon as her elbows hit his back. Jesufon molds his face, his forehead wrinkles and he looks older. He seems hurt.

"*Ode,*" he mumbles, and I am sure the expletive is for the young bus conductor who already looks cursed from many fights or maybe from a hit by one of the lorries we are after this morning. But almost all the yellow bus conductors in Lagos look like him, with isolated teeth that one could count all at a swift glance, and ears that look like someone bit them off thinking they were roasted *ponmo.* Jesufon stands and draws Jane up by the hand.

"We can ask him where we can catch a lorry," Jesufon screams. "These *agberos* know everything and everywhere in this *Eko.*"

"Okay," I manage to say while I pant with drops of sweat running through scattered tracks on my face. I try to wipe them off with my forefinger and let them fall on the tar by a swipe. "Can you please ask any of the other ones? I don't like this one."

Jesufon does not hear me, or maybe he is acting like he doesn't.

"*Níbo lati ma rí àwon okò ñla?* We urgently need a lorry," he says to the young conductor, the one who had just stopped him and made him fall on the tar with Zinwhe. I am not surprised he speaks little Yoruba. He has been to the city with Yoruba boys a few more times than most of his peers.

"*Âwon okò nlá pò ní Ojota. Wón ma n kúrò ní àáró,*" the young conductor replies in a rusty voice, and the smell of local gin oozes from his mouth. It smells like *kparaga*, as Anonye would call it when Papa returned home after going out to drink with his friends. Zinwhe forces her two fingers into her nostrils and corks both openings. She must have smelt it. It must have reminded her of Papa and the hurts we feel each day because we are aware he will never return to us.

"He says we can catch a lorry at Ojota. But we have to get there first," Jesufon screams. He is smiling, and his voice cracks. He stammers a few more words, grabs me by both arms and shakes me as if he is trying so hard to wake me from a deep sleep.

He turns back to face the conductor, "*Sé Ojota lo n lo?*"

"*Ehn! Wo lé,*" the young conductor yells. Jesufon rushes into the back end of the bus. Zinwhe follows, I follow. I am always the last, not because Zinwhe is faster. I am the last because I always want to run behind her, to watch over her, to make sure she is safe. We are Gunuvi. Lagos is sometimes not accommodating to us. Lagos is most times a scary place for us. I always have to be behind my little sister to watch over her.

Zinwhe became my responsibility the day Otodo-Gbame fell in the hands of the police, the uniformed officers who came with bulldozers and guns. We were jumping into Papa's *dadihun*, the one he went with for fishing, when Anonye started yelling and threatening to upset the canoe and let everyone in the water.

"Zinwhe!" she screamed. "Where is my Zinwhe?"

We had lost Zinwhe while we were in a hurry to leave the

settlement. Several gunshots were heard in the air, and many families surged into the main sea, paddling with their belongings, running to safety. Our canoes, all together, created ripples in the sea and the ripples became tides. And all the canoes rocked in different rhythms, up and down. A few more gunshots and Anonye cried even more. A cry I could not hold. I left the canoe and dived into the water, and swam my way back, throwing one arm after the other. The sounds of the water, the gunshots, and the falling apart of corrugated zinc sheets and plywood that were once the roofs and walls of our homes, and the cries of many, were all I heard as I dipped my head in and out of the smelly waters.

As I climbed into our home which was yet to fall, I didn't see Zinwhe. She was not at home. It was Papa I met lying on the floor of the bedroom with a pool of blood all around him and blood still gushing out. He choked. His chest forced upwards and fell, and rose again and fell. More blood gushed. And he became flat and stopped moving. I held his hand and tried to pull him to sit up, but Papa was heavy and cold. He had lost blood, so much blood than I ever thought he could have in him. I bent down to touch his neck but the roof of our home gave way and the sun threw in light. I looked up to see but the light blinded me. And then the sound became clearer; the sound of destruction, of things falling apart. It was the sound that went from house to house, from shanty to shanty, and erased all we knew of what were our homes. It was our turn now, and it became clearer and noisier. I made my way outside, marched a weak floor and fell into the waters. Everything became dark; even my mind.

"Zannu," Zinwhe says, softly, in my ear. "We are coming

down here. Jesufon has paid the man."

"Where is he?" I ask. This place looks different.

"I'm out already," Jesufon shouts. "Run out of that bus. No one waits for anyone in Eko."

I jump off the bus and stand next to Zinwhe and Jesufon. The day is brighter now and darkness is almost lost. We stand under the concrete footbridge. Jesufon stands firm. His face is dry and white, and his wrists and knuckles. Jesufon is dark in complexion and has short legs. His chests are small. I wonder how he has all that courage. Zinwhe is dry and white too. And I look at my hands. They are white also.

"Run!" Jesufon yells. "Run, both of you! See the lorry. Run faster than your legs!"

And we run as fast as we can, after the big truck that drove ahead of us. We run until we spend all our sweat. Jesufon catches up with the truck, holds the metal bucket and climbs. He stops and waits. He lets out his hand and I grab him. He pulls me up to him. I climb above him, jump and fall into the bucket of the truck. Zinwhe jumps in next. And then Jesufon. We are panting. My throat is dry and gummy. I wait patiently for saliva to soak up my throat. It doesn't happen so quickly. The truck is empty, but for a few cow dungs.

And finally, we leave Lagos, Iya Ahisi, and Anonye, with this smell.

WE LOSE THE THINGS WE LOVE

&

There was something similar to the day Zosi was born and the day she returned to Makoko with those white people. I was eight years old and at home when Mama started screaming and rubbing her stomach in a circular motion at a very fast pace. Papa had just climbed out of his canoe and was already seated on the handcrafted bamboo stool in the room, waiting for Mama to serve him his favorite *eko* and *banga soup*. I had stepped out to the front platform because Papa said something about children being disrespectful if they insisted on sitting and watching their parents wipe every trace of soup from the bowl.

I was outside, watching the women who traded detergents and spices inside their *tojihun*, paddling from one house to the other and yelling the names of their goods at the top of their voices. I was outside watching the kids play inside their small canoes, and sometimes jump from one wooden canoe to the other in excitement. I saw the canoes that collided and danced, with their paddlers moving in rhythm and finding balance with their long bamboo sticks thrust deep into the smelly water, and the much older people who heaved off smaller boats by younger people. These are the life and sound of Makoko. We saw no birds in the morning singing us to consciousness, nor did we hear the crows of the chickens. We did not hear the stamps of feet from the romping about of little children. These were all we saw and heard in our community.

Mama yelled even before she was done with Papa's food.

Papa was the one who held her and lifted her from the ground, brought her into his canoe and paddled her to the clinic as she screamed and called on the different gods of the waters and land. I was at home when Zosi was born later in the evening. Papa came home, smiling and singing the fisherman's song of conquest. He danced and paced about our little bedroom, and all I heard was that a baby girl was the gift from the goddess of the waters, the one who gave us the fishes in the seas.

"Zosu," Papa said, "You now have a sister, a very beautiful sister. Your mother has made all of us proud. I cannot dance enough. I need to call my sister to let her know."

"Is she *oyinbo?*" I managed to ask. I wasn't sure of what to say or ask. I didn't know what to tell a father of a newborn. "Is she yellow, Papa?"

"Yellow keh?" he stopped his dancing. "And where would the yellow come from? We are too dark to be bleached, your mother and I."

"Okay, Papa," I finally said and lowered my head to the ground. But I felt the cuddle of laughter and beauty in my soul, and my lips curved into an upper arch. I thought about being alone at home all the time. This meant it was all over.

An Ofa oracle was raised for Zosi, and Papa said it was for us to know her destiny, what the future held for her. This happened for a few more days before Mama and Zosi returned home to live with us, and the cries of Zosi was all that we heard every night for many months after. I never heard Papa mention what her destiny was, nor did I hear him mention that she would grow to become a nurse on the mainland, would one day bring white people to

Makoko to help teach our young women how to do better jobs, and also fight the government to let us live and fish in our waters.

I had just made it to thirty years a few weeks before and had gone to visit Mama with some of the best fishes I had caught when I heard that the Hounon had visited the family house twice that morning when all the fishermen were yet to return from the deep sea. Mama said he climbed into the house and into the bedroom and was smiling and shaking hands with Papa.

"Zosi is coming to Makoko with white people," Mama said. She was making banana and *klaku* for me in her special pot because she knew it was my special dish.

"That's quite nice of her," I said to Mama. I stared at the family picture of Papa, Mama, me, and Zosi which hung on the wall of the bedroom next to where my parents rested their heads. It was shot by Kpeton, the photographer, a couple of months after Zosi's birth. "I'm sure they are her colleagues at the clinic in the mainland."

"I think so too," Mama yelled from the kitchen. "Zosi is a very lovable girl. They all love her at the clinic. You know I've been to the clinic?"

"I know, Mama. You're quite popular there."

"Yes, I am," Mama chuckled. "I am the proud mother of the youngest nurse in that clinic. They treat me like a queen."

"Have you met the white people?" I asked Mama, just to keep her company and talking.

"Oh, no," she replied. "I've never met them. But I've heard about them."

"Great," I said to her. "We must prepare for them. They need to enjoy their stay."

Mama said the Hounon had already prepared for their reception at his *hounhonu*. She said it was rare for a traditional ruler to paddle that much, that early morning, to the house of an ordinary man if he was not hatching a huge celebration for his visitors.

"Zosi will first visit the house with her friends," Mama yelled again. "After that, they can all paddle to the *hounhonu*."

Then she kept quiet, and all that moved around the house was the smell of the meal she prepared in her very small and sacred kitchen. A few minutes later, Papa climbed into the house. He had gone to the pool office to play coupon. He seemed to have very little to say that morning as he pulled off his shirt and hung it on a nail on the wall next to the stereo that never worked.

"*Na afon do*," I greeted him.

"*Lo fon gangi*," he replied. "And how is your family?"

"Very fine, Papa," I said to him. "*Na ale do?*"

"I'm well," Papa answered. Then he complained of back pain, which he said was attached to becoming old. He went to meet Mama in the kitchen and said very little to her before finding rest in his bed. It wasn't long before he began snoring away the stress of the morning and easing the odor of gin into the air of the bedroom. The hairs on his chest were all white and quite countable if I had tried to count them. His nipples were shrunk and dry.

"Is he sleeping already?" Mama asked from the kitchen. "Is your father asleep?"

I didn't say a word to Mama.

"That's how he sleeps these days," Mama continued. "Since Zosi called and told him to stop fishing, he just sleeps like old palm oil."

* * * * * *

Zosi did not come the day everyone waited for her to show up with the white people. She didn't show up at the house. She also didn't show up at the *hounhonu*. The Hounon waited for days and stopped waiting, and everyone carried on with their lives.

One Thursday evening, I was told that I had been summoned by the Hounon at the house. I paddled as fast as my arms could and pushed my canoe forward with the bamboo stick. In no time, I was at the house. I was tying my canoe to the platform when I heard a cry in the house. I quickly climbed in and saw Zosi and Mama yelling and throwing themselves to the floor, while the Hounon was sitting on the bed and resting his jaws on his palms. Papa lay lifeless in the bed. He was dead and cold.

Papa had died after he had gone to bed at night. He never woke up. He never woke to paddle to the pool office to check some games. He never woke to sail to Kpeton's bar for some shots of local gin. It was just his cold body with his bare chest and Mama and Zosi that I saw in the bedroom while the Hounon stood up and whispered something in my ear before he left. I did not hear his words, but I was sure they were words of consolation as he patted my back before he left.

A couple of months had gone by and Papa had been buried in Badagry when Zosi sailed into Makoko with two white women. There was tension in the air as Gunuvis, in their hundreds, surged into Makoko for refuge. The government had unleashed the brutality of the police on them and their homes were being destroyed. Someone said they heard so many gunshots in the night. Another one said someone was shot dead.

"Who chases people out of their houses at night?" I asked

whoever came to share the sad news with me. But no one cared to provide the answer. No one knew exactly why they came in the night.

"They are selling Otodo-Gbame to the rich."

"They have already sold Otodo-Gbame."

"They'll fill the waters with sand and build for the rich."

"They'll sell at high prices and buy big cars, and send their children abroad."

"This is quite unjust. The people committed no crime."

"They did! In Lagos, it is a crime to be poor."

We heard many sides of the story in those days. However, Zosi had visited the Hounon with what seemed to be the right story of how the people of Otodo-Gbame had been forced out of their community and were divided among the many settlements of our people. The Hounon had summoned every young man in front of the palace and while we sat in our canoes, he gave out instructions on how we were to protect the community from elimination by the government. We were to be careful about how we spoke to journalists, and the NGOs, and the many visitors that brought free lunch for the children. We were to keep our lifestyles and tradition sacred, and not share any information concerning our waters with anyone that was not one of us. We were to welcome the Gunuvis from Otodo-Gbame and support them in erecting new homes for them and their children.

"Rose wishes to teach our women how to make things for themselves," Zosi said.

We were together at the family house to see Mama. She had been complaining of pains in her joints, and Zosi said she had rheumatism.

"What sort of things is she teaching them to make?" I asked.

"To make things," she replied. "They'll learn to make household things like soap, beads and many other decorative things they can sell in the town."

"Our women are more interested in smoking fish and paddling around Makoko with little goods," Mama said. She sat in her bamboo recliner, the one Papa had made with his hands.

"Mama, they would love what Rose and Catherine are here to teach them," Zosi continued. "Not all Makoko women should smoke fish for a living, even if the entire Lagos needed all the fishes in the ocean. A few of them would wish to learn other trades. And you should bring your wife, Zosu. She will learn a lot from this."

"Mahutin would be interested, I know for sure," I said to her. "She has been talking so much about you lately, and admires everything you do."

"All the young women are proud of Zosi," Mama said. "She is on everyone's lips. Everyone in Makoko."

Mama smiled. She then rested her back on the recliner and closed her eyes. She breathed like she suddenly fell asleep. But her eyes blinked at intervals. I looked a little at Mama, and then at Zosi who slid through a collection of old photos which she took from Mama's drawer.

They were the same photos I loved checking out anytime I visited. They were Papa's very old photographs at Badagry when he was an intern with a popular Gunuvi sculptor. Papa had mentioned his name a lot of times, but it refused to be inscribed in my memory. Papa's photographs were not the only ones in the collection. Our photographs were there too, our baby photographs,

Zosi and I. Zosi saw one of those, lifted it to her face and smiled. And she turned to look at me. We smiled, but we said nothing afterward. She had grown so much. And her influence in Makoko had been commended by everyone. I was going to let Mahutin know about her program with the white women. And she was going to be trained and become influential herself.

In the morning, someone started the screaming. Someone started the yelling and name-calling. It was a man who started yelling, a young man. He raised his voice so loud that it wasn't long before others joined him, yelling in their canoes, paddling to the *hounhonu* and singing noisily in different rhythms. They were singing Gunuvi songs of solidarity. They were songs of togetherness, especially in times of an honest war against oppressors from the government and our enemies. It was too early in the morning, as just a few fishermen had sailed their *dadihun* to the main sea; while very many others straightened and untangled their nets in readiness to set sail. It was not too early for the chickens to crow—though chickens did not crow in Makoko because we had none. Birds did not sing too. But we knew early mornings. We woke once the sky welcomes a little light.

"They are infiltrators from the government," someone yelled from the crowd of canoes. I could not make out the face as I stood up to look through the crowd from the back. But he sounded like the first voice to yell that morning.

"We have all the information we need," he continued as everyone gave him a nudge. "They are done with Otodo Gbame. Now they want us too."

"They say we are criminals," someone else yelled from the crowd.

26

"And prostitutes," another joined in. This time, a woman.

"But we will not let it happen," the leader declared. "Makoko is as strong as the strong wind that pushes down the *Iroko*. We shall push them down."

Everyone started talking and murmuring, saying things to themselves and the people next to them. Someone by my canoe, a man, said many things to me that I didn't listen to. I didn't want to listen to what he said. I was afraid. I was scared that Zosi was the one who brought the white women to Makoko. I was scared that she never knew what harm she had caused by letting infiltrators into our waters. I was worried about her, and about Mama who would give up on happiness if someone told her that Zosi brought spies into Makoko. I had to force myself out of the crowd of canoes, and find my way to Mama before anyone would get to tell her all that was happening, I thought. And as the Hounon picked a few heads from the crowd and invited them into his *hounhonu*, I pushed aside a few canoes and forced myself out of the crowd, towards the family house. As I dipped my bamboo into the water and pushed forward, darts of early morning sweats spotted on my arms and soaked my faded green singlet. Deep snuffles erupted from my nose and drop sweat splattered from nostrils and landed on my chest.

The many wooden houses I passed erupted fumes from their rooftops and Makoko smelt of smoked tilapia. It reminded me that I hadn't gone to check on the net traps I set the night before. It reminded me that Makoko had scantily fished that morning and that everything had gone wrong already. I remembered Zosi and wished she remained in the mainland. I wished she knew the white women were from the government. I wished she never met them again. And I wished the Hounon knew her mind was pure for Makoko.

At the family house, Papa's old canoe stopped mine and I tied mine to it. I stepped into it and found my way to the stairs. I climbed out of the old boat and into the family house. The wooden door was not locked. As I pushed the door, it opened and hinged towards the right. The bedroom was quiet; dead quiet. No living creature could have been in the bedroom. Not even the moth or other creepers which ate the wood of the house when everywhere was quiet. Not even the bed bugs which Mama always complained about. Everywhere was quiet and dead, and nothing moved.

Mama sat, unmoved, in her bamboo recliner. She sat there without turning or saying a word to me, without blinking, as she did whenever she wanted us to know she needed to sleep. Her eyes were wide open like she never feared anything would perch on them. She never turned to see if I was coming close to her. I wasn't coming close. I stood close to the bed frame, while my knees trembled and every space and walls caved in. The room became smaller and the walls trampled towards me. Mama sat down with her hands thrown wide apart, quiet, cold and sleeping the kind of sleep I knew she was never going to wake from. I walked past mama, into her kitchen, and quenched the oven. I let the smell of smoked fish into my nostrils, and soon it filled my chest. Tears clog my eyes.

WE CAN'T BEAT THESE THINGS

Checkmate jumps the little gate at Woolwich Arsenal Train Station in a haste to join the DLR to Bank Station. It is his little way of telling me that he owns the entire city of London and that he's the only person I can hang out with. He did something like this yesterday in the station at Heathrow Airport, where he ran past a gate before it could shut. He did not swipe on the sensor with his Oyster card, although he took time to purchase a top-up of five pounds before he spoke to me for the first time, "Welcome to London, you bush boy."

I wonder if he must have lost his card, or maybe it is his ultimate right to do whatever pleases him. Everyone is passing us. No one bothers to stop and rebuke him for passing illegally. Everyone is just moving zigzag, fast-fast, hand swinging up and down, sounds of shoe soles here and there like people are nailing concrete nails into corrugated asbestos sheets. No one looks at Checkmate. No one looks at me. I look at them but, they act like my stare doesn't sting.

My nickname is Sting. That is the only thing I gained for passing through a neighborhood secondary school where everyone knew everyone, and parents knew parents because they were neighbors, and their children played soccer together on a grassless pitch in the same neighborhood secondary school. Everyone knew everyone because everyone worshipped in the same mushroom church in a small classroom, in the same neighborhood secondary school. The same church that was led by that skinny pastor who said he resurrected four days after he had died. No one believed his testimony. Not even Mama who was the leader of the women; the same women who were Checkmate's mother, Trouble's mother, and David and Goliath's mother. No one believed him.

In Slum Estate, all we needed was a church and since the orthodox priests avoided bringing the gospel to our neighborhood, we all gathered and anointed Pastor Giver Receiver as our priest because he said he died and woke up after four days, a day longer than Jesus stayed.

"Who has stayed dead more than Jesus if not Giver?" Mama asked. "Who even has the guts to say he did?"

Checkmate knows Pastor Giver Receiver very well. Pastor Giver Receiver said Checkmate stole the church offering from the vicarage while the church leaders were having a meeting in the church hall. He announced in church that Checkmate would be made to sit on the last row during church services so that the Holy Spirit would have been exhausted before it got to Checkmate at the back. It was his punishment for stealing from the Lord. The women turned and stared in shock at Checkmate. Mama turned and stared angrily at me, ridges formed tightly on her forehead. Checkmate ran out of the church before Pastor Giver Receiver could finish his judgment on him and he never returned to church again. We never returned to church again; not me, not Trouble, not David and Goliath. We smoked cigarettes on Sundays and began to smoke weed later on. We became bad boys.

"These dogs don't even bite," Checkmate says to me. He must have caught my eyes staring at the big dog sitting on the floor of the train close to a lady who looks Asian but speaks English like she has lived here all her life.

"Nothing bites here in London. They just move around like *mumu*. They say nothing to you. The system keeps controlling them remotely."

The Asian lady turns her glare towards us. She must have heard Checkmate. I smile at her to show her we are friendly people. She does not smile back at me. She turns back to the Asian boy sitting next to her. Her dog drools on the floor of the train. It cannot control those fluids from dropping. It looks like a bulldog. It is not smiling.

"But dogs don't share things with humans," I say to Checkmate.

"You're just a bush boy. These people don't know the difference between dogs and humans. Not even pigeons."

At Canning Town Station, the Asian lady stands to walk away and her dog follows her. I watch them as they step out of the train. I guess Checkmate is watching too. The Asian boy does not stand to leave the train. He must be watching too, probably watching us watch the lady and the dog.

"They love these animals more than they love you fucking Africans," Checkmate says.

I am still watching the lady and the dog. The doors shut. No one shuts them. They shut by themselves.

"They think these animals they kiss have more brains than we do."

"Their father!" I reply Checkmate.

I don't like what he just said. I hate humiliation, not when it comes from the white guy whose forefathers stole our oil and sold them to build their nations.

"They are all animals, can't you see?"

Checkmate doesn't answer me. He goes ahead with his story about how he was the only black man on a train and every other person refused to get close to him. He tells me about how a guy kept staring furiously at him because he was the reason why all of them were standing. I find his story boring and unbelievable.

We arrive at Bank Station and the train stops for us to alight. As we leave the station, I think of all the wonders of this new place. I think of many things—from the black man who slept all through on the train to the boy who kept kissing this girl without shame, or respect for the older people on the train. I wonder if the sleeping man worked two or more jobs and was tired after everything. I fear he would pass his station and get missing somewhere else.

There are people standing and reading books in front of the train station, under the summer sun, close to men and women smoking cigarettes and drinking coffee in front of a café that had pastries clearly showcased you can see them through this clear glass window pane. Then the red buses drive by, the buses that have many words written on them. There are electronic numbers on them. Checkmate knows the number he wants. As soon as Bus 48 stops in front of us, Checkmate rushes in. I run after him. Checkmate brings out his Oyster card from his wallet, swipes on the indicator light close to the driver, and the green light shows. I do the same. I am now becoming a Londoner like Checkmate; like the white guys, the Londoners themselves. We do not stand. We climb to the upper cabin and find our seats in front, before the windscreen.

"We'll meet him at the hospital," Checkmate says. "He's in

charge. He'll employ you at once. There's no time to waste. You should start making your own pounds."

I can't wait to start making pounds sterling. I can't wait to start sending money to Mama, Papa and Chibuike, I mutter to myself. I stare shortly at Checkmate. I don't want him to catch me staring at him. I suddenly have this fear, this respect, for him.

We're in front of what Checkmate says is the hospital. It does not look like one. It does not look like our General Hospital with many bungalows spread all around the compound with the Pharmacy close to the gate, next to the morgue, the offices; and the wards which were over a mile away from the laboratory and the only theatre. It does not have old rickety vans which no one drove and which served as ambulances, all around the compound as if the mechanics used the land as a workshop. St. Anthony Hospital looks like a five-star hotel, and I wonder if people ever get sick in London. There are real trees with real green leaves planted beautifully all around. I'm sure they didn't just grow by themselves.

People are not just walking in and out, and about, or loitering all over the place. People are not in front of the gate, crying like everyone in their village just died. There's no gate even. We walk into the hospital after crossing the minor road which is bigger than our Tetlow Road, which is the major road that leads to our Slum Estate. We're crossing the road with no cars honking, and no one swearing that *Amadioha* would scatter our heads for not being fast.

Checkmate's friend is a Zimbabwean. He's not Zimbabwean in the way he talks, not like the way most Zimbabweans speak English like they are spitting out large molds of *fufu*. He is more

33

British than Checkmate. Checkmate is not British in any way. He allows us to sit down on cushioned chairs. It is not his office. It is the changing room for all the hospital cleaning staff, and he is the boss of the cleaners. He does not need an office. All he needs are good shoes to help him move around the entire building to check what the other cleaners are doing, he said.

St. Anthony Hospital is not for us. We're only the house-keeping staff. St. Anthony Hospital is for those drunken youths who, after a fierce weekend, got into a fight and tore each other's skin with the jagged blades of broken bottles. It is for the white boy who was beaten to vegetables by some bad boys in his neighborhood. They fought because of this girl and that girl, and those girls. The hospital is for the kidney patient and the old white man with a heart disease.

It is for those Nigerian politicians who are always here because they have headaches and diarrhea that will never be cured. They come here in droves, themselves, their wives, their children and their personal assistants. They lodge in private wards, with cable television, internet, and room service. They have visitors every day. Their visitors come with nothing but leave the hospital carrying bags, *Ghana-must-go* bags. I know what they carry in those bags. I know they carry money; money they stole from their constituencies, money they stole from their states, money they stole from Nigeria.

Nigeria is a careless woman, very careless. Everyone steals from her. She leaves her purse for all to see. She cannot account for how much she has in her account. The ones she trusts her future in their hands are the ones who keep pruning her best from her. Her friends, those women called Britain and France and Netherlands and China, and the almighty America, all welcome to their houses those who steal from her. They don't let her know they have her best with them. They only use her best and send leftovers to her. Then they run to CNN and BBC and CCTV. They let the other women know all they have given to Nigeria. They're not good friends. But they're beautiful women because they have good mirrors to look at themselves while dressing every morning. Nigeria cannot afford to buy a mirror to appreciate how beautiful she is and can become. It is because of men like Senator Onyema that Nigeria cannot afford to buy her own mirror.

"Oh you're an Igbo man," Senator Onyema says to me. He sat on a fluffy sofa, close to the bed, his eyes fixed on something he's watching on television.

"Nnamdi. Nice. Good to know you didn't change your name the way our people do whenever they travel abroad."

Senator Onyema starts to giggle, and I wonder why he is laughing. Is he laughing at me, at my name, or at those Nigerians who change their names here in London because they want the white man to know they also have English names?

I know Senator Onyema Mbachu too well, more than he knows himself. He is the senator in charge of Orlu Zone, which is where I come from. He is the man Papa called dreadful names because he has refused to step down since he won the election in 1999.

"Onyema this, Onyema this. Bastard. Fool. Criminal. Illiterate. He will soon die," Papa would curse.

Papa hated this fat and ugly man sitting here before me like he hated Chief Ralph who stole the mercury in the neighborhood transformer and sold it to some northerners in Kano. I throw white linen over the bed and tuck it in.

"Don't clip the pillow with your lower jaw while tucking into the case. You can pick up one skin disease or the other," Ivor says at every morning's toolbox meeting where all the cleaners prepare for the day's housekeeping. I know Ivor is always trying to be polite. I know he fears more that we do not infect the patients than he fears us getting sick from the patients and their different illnesses.

This morning, I'm sure Senator Onyema is not a sick man—no eczema, no ringworm, no chickenpox. I clip the pillow between my lower jaw and my collar bones, flip the case to allow air inflate it, and slid the pillow into the case. Then I close the open end with the flap, just like one would do with an envelope. I pick up the second pillow and do the same.

"Are you a student?" Senator Onyema asks. He pulls up his singlet to his chest to reveal a mound of flesh that is his stomach.

"No, sir," I reply him. I do not want to look at this man who stole all the money the state government had given him to build a stadium for the sports-loving youths. I do not look at him.

"You work here?" he asks again.

"No, I don't. Yes, of course, I do, dummy," I want to tell him. But I can't be rude to a man who controls over half a million Orlu people and their money.

"Yes, I do," I say to him instead. "I will soon raise enough money for school in Aberdeen. I need to work for that money, sir."

"Exactly," he's now grinning, his teeth are brown from chewing kola nuts. "That's what our people lack. The will to survive. No one wants to work. Everyone is talking about allocations. Allocation this, allocation that. But I tell them, work. Money does not fall from heaven as if it will replace the rains. Onyemachukwu will not give you money because he does not have it."

I am quiet. I say nothing. The senator is back watching the television. Someone in CNN is talking about a silly boy who just butchered a soldier in Woolwich. The boy is British but black because his parents are Nigerians. They have video clips of him yelling, shoving his bloody hands on the screen. There's a black lady he is trying to explain to what his reasons are; why he, first of all, ran the white soldier over with his car before butchering him into parts with the tomahawk that he's still holding in his hands.

"Afghanistan! United Kingdom! United States! Islam! Allah!" those are all I hear him scream.

People are all around but far away from where he is, watching him rant and shout. Only this black lady, who looks like she has a husband and children of her own, stands before him; and yes, the cameraman whose lens beam what we see.

"Who's this idiot?" Senator Onyema now looks provoked. He stands up from the sofa, rests his hands on his waist, and watches the television as if he will see through the device into the actual street, as if the extremist will feel the heat of his gaze and cry of the heat.

"Extremist my foot," he says.

I'm glad I thought of the word before the honorable senator could pour it out. Extremist.

"Now they say he's Nigerian because he has done something inhuman. I bet you this idiot has never been to Nigeria all his useless life."

I am sweeping the floor of the bathroom and the bedroom. Senator Onyema is busy moving from one edge of the room to another to permit me to sweep off every bit of dust without him obstructing me. I am happy I can control such a man, such a man who comes to Orlu with various kinds of SUVs in a convoy, and mobile police officers clearing his path with whips planted on the backs of drivers or passersby who dared hinder his movement. I am glad that the next time I call home I'll tell Papa, Mama, and Chibuike, especially Chibuike, that I have Senator Onyema Mbachu's remote control in my pocket. Chibuike will not believe it. He thinks the senator is a god or something close to a god who has the power to punish the disloyal with fire and brimstone.

I finish sweeping. I listen to the trickling sound of the liquid disinfectant as it descends in drops into the mopping bucket. Then I shut my eyelids and lift my nostrils. I inhale the scent that is now in the air. I smile. I smile because it reminds me of home. It reminds me of Mama and her cleaning. How she would carry a little gallon of disinfectant to the toilet in the morning before the first cock would crow, before the stars became shy, before anyone would wake to fetch water for bathing. Mama would scrub the cement screed floor of the toilet with a hard brush, her knees resting on the floor. She would wash off the dirt with water, and then spray a locally made air freshener all over the bathroom and toilet.

"*Ehn ehn*, no more germs. I hate germs," she would say before leaving for the kitchen to cook for the family.

Senator Onyema is now at the balcony, waiting for me to be done with the mopping of the floors, for the scent to go down a bit

and for me to spray the deodorizer. He is outside smoking cigarettes, butt after butt, and carelessly dropping them on the floor
of the balcony. He is smoking at the balcony, even with all the
obvious signs and cautions on all the walls of the hospital which
say *DO NOT SMOKE* and *SMOKING PROHIBITED*. The wind is mer-
ciful. It pushes the fumes and the odor of the cigarettes out in the
open. He is smoking our country in the open, butt after butt, rel-
ishing every inhalation before allowing the chaffs to whiff in the
air. He's dropping what is left of my country on the floor, quench-
ing her last light with his right foot.

I stand, waiting to tell him that I have finished with his
room. He does not wait for me to call him. He is also done with his
last stick of cigarette. He returns to the room. For the first time, I
look into his eyes. I look at the figure of the man that took Papa's
only land because they wanted to build a community clinic on it.
That is what Papa said the day he rushed into the living room,
happy like he just won the lotto, holding his phone in one hand.

"His P.A. just called me," Papa said.

"P.A.?" Mama asked. "Whose P.A?"

"Onyema's P.A," Papa said. "I agreed to give them the land
close to St. James."

"You what?"

"Yes, I've finally agreed. And we won't have to pay for these
kids' costly school fees anymore. The council will pay those fees.
I made him know that!"

"I don't believe you, Julius," Mama was between shouting
and whispers like she wanted her words to nail into Papa's ears
but also didn't want anyone else to hear her scream at her husband like that.

"Are we the only ones with that size of land? Can't Onyema go and look for others who have bigger portions? Why does he think he can always deceive you, Julius? Ehn, Julius?"

"No one is deceiving Julius this time, *Nne*. Julius has made known his demands. This time, they shall be met. And we will also benefit from the free medical care that clinic would offer our people."

"But you don't stay in the village," Mama said.

"Yes, we don't stay in the village, but it is ours. The village is ours," Papa replied Mama.

I pretended to be busy reading the newspaper. Papa brought one back every day and he made it a law that we read those papers daily. I wondered what Papa meant by the village is ours like we had just paid and bought the entire Akata village and the farmlands and the people and the animals in it. I did not give it much thought. This was Papa. This was how he talked whenever he was so sure of something, something that would definitely happen. This was how he talked before his company sent him his promotion letter and an official car to go with it. This was how Papa talked whenever he was very sure of something.

After two years, Papa was wrong. Senator Onyema Mbachu had built a castle on Papa's land and made it his country home. Papa's heart shattered like China ceramic bowl. Papa employed a lawyer, and the lawyer grew fat on his money. And when Papa ran out of money, the short, now fat, lawyer ran to Senator Onyema, sat by his footstool and ate from the crumbs dropped by the senator. That was how Papa lost his land, lost his pride, lost his smile, and kept paying our tuition fees.

"What did the doctors say about your illness?" I am bold to

ask him. I forgot to add "Sir" and I am glad I didn't.

"Oh, nothing that serious," he replies. "I probably just need to rest for a couple of days before I return to Abuja. I'm glad I'm here. There's madness over there."

"That sounds good," I say.

"Yes, it is good. All good," he says and slumps into the bed I have made with clinical craftsmanship for the third time that morning.

"Where are you from?" he asks me.

I do not answer him. I act like his last words flew with the wind like the fume of cigarettes. He does not ask any further. Then I hear a knock on the door.

"Oh, that must be Toby," Senator Onyema says. "They called me from the front desk that he is around. You must leave now. Toby is my representative here in London. We have important things to talk about."

"Not a problem, sir," I say to him. "I'm done with the room. I'll be on my way."

"Have this." He pulls out a brown leather suitcase from under his bed. He unlocks it and hands out some wads of pounds sterling before me.

"Not to bother," my mouth wouldn't let me spit those words. I take the notes from his hands and head straight to the door. This is my share of Nigeria!

I see a tall man waiting in front of the door when I open the door to leave. He looks Nigerian. He looks African. He is well-dressed in a black suit like today is his wedding day and he is ready to drive down to the church to take his bride.

"Hi," I say to him.

He does not say a word to me as I step out of the room and walk along the passage without turning to observe him a second time. I had just completed my last hour at work today. I am sitting on this concrete bench in front of St. Anthony, thinking what happened in that room. I am thinking how come I did not notice the suitcase under the bed. I am thinking of what Ivor would have said to me if I told him I did not see the suitcase under the bed: "How many times will I tell you this, Nandi? Clean, clean, clean everywhere. Sweep, sweep, sweep everywhere. Under the sofa, under the table, move the drip stand and all those machines, sweep under the bed."

* * * * *

Kate is Zimbabwean. She doesn't have that accent that makes you fear she would one day spit out her tongue just because she spoke English. But she looks Zimbabwean, biggest behind that vibrates at every step she takes; and finely molded chest, like a sculptor carefully carved and glued them in the right places. She is black. She is fond of me. She is also done with her hours at the laboratory. She is out here, sitting on this concrete bench with me, waiting for the sun to come down, waiting for water to drain the last flake of snack in our throats down to our bowels, waiting for time, waiting for the bus, waiting for a destination.

I am thinking about Checkmate. He had angrily walked out on me barely two weeks after I started the cleaning job. We had met to have dinner after work. While we waited in line for our turn, a young white female, who couldn't have been more than 15 years old, had called the attention of the restaurant's supervisor. According to her, Checkmate had this nauseating foul smell and they wanted him to leave the queue and even the restaurant. Checkmate was livid! I tried to calm him down but he got angry the more, called me a betrayal who could not stand up for his own brother. He left the restaurant with a firm resolve never to be so humiliated again in his life. I never saw him again since then. I sense he has gone to Aberdeen to work in the oil fields, or he is getting involved in internet and credit card fraud to achieve his goal to get rich.

I am thinking about Nigeria in the hands of Senator Onyema. I am thinking about tonight with Kate. I am wondering if I should bother about these things.

Things That Start Small But Sweet

WHEN THINGS CHANGE

᪥

C harlie is not his name; not even his English name. He does not have an English name but is determined not to die without one. Charlie is a name he cleverly chose because no one in Britain, not even his old white lady, the lady in her eighties, had the tongue to call out his real name, Mgbeahuruike. He then reasoned that being namesake with the Prince of Wales would make the Brits love and adore him like he was tea.

The white lady cannot, today, remember the names of her two sons, the ones who left her as soon as they were sure they were eighteen. She is yet to see them or find where they are. The only thing or person she sees these days is Charlie, the Nigerian boy in his twenties, whom she is in love with. She is sure her sons are no more in Coventry.

"No, not my Coventry," she sounded so sure to Charlie. To Charlie, that doesn't matter as much as his work and residence permit papers. It doesn't matter to Charlie more than the new house in Leamington Spa which she just paid off the mortgage. This house matters to Charlie more than the house in Coventry.

"Who would wish to stay back at Coventry with the old vintage stench of Sally after she's dead and gone?" Charlie confided in me while we got drunk in a pub at Canning Town.

Today, a week after, Charlie calls me.

"She's sick again," he sounds happy over the phone. "This time the doctor says she won't survive it. A woman as old as eighty-four years will never survive a heart attack."

"How about your papers?" I ask him. "What will become of you?"

"I'm her next-of-kin, isn't it? Who cares about residence permit this time! Very soon, I'll own a house in this fucking United Kingdom and all will be history."

"Lucky you!" I say. I'm not sure that I meant congratulations.

He giggles. It was irritating to my ears. "You're not smart, Ike. I told you to do the same several years ago. You chose to be a scholar, First degree, Second degree, Ph.D. How much?"

"How do you mean?" I meant to tell him "Fuck you".

"How much have you earned after all your London education? You can't even send money home."

"But I called Mama last Thursday."

"You called your mother last Thursday," he sounds like he means to ask me a question. I don't answer him.

"And today is what?"

"Thursday," I answer him this time.

"It's one week today and you're yet to send her the money you promised her for her business," he says, reminding me of my failure to provide for my mother. I keep mute.

"Fuck the schools. Get a white lady and go for your stay," he concluded offhandedly.

It's Friday morning. I did not find sleep last night, I did not look for it. Charlie made me hate sleep. It was intentional. He knows I love my sleep. He feels I sleep too much and that is why I am yet to make a free pound since I dropped out of Architecture in Nigeria and ran to London for a better education under white professors whom I thought would have white beards like Wole

Soyinka. He feels I was disappointed when I got to London and found that the universities here are not as big as ten classroom blocks, not as big as the University of Benin. What's in the size of a university if it cannot make brains? I tell myself as I embrace this morning. But I am disappointed in many things, in many things that brought me here.

"Chibuike won the councillorship election," Mama told me last week when we spoke over the phone. "Your younger brother is a real brave man. He won that old idiot who thought he was the only one in this ward who knew how to rig elections. He's now surprised at how your brother did it."

I remember Mama's words and how I heard Chibuike in the background, chuckling all his lungs out. I exhale, wondering if I can release all the air in my chest. Then I wonder what made Mama call him "a real brave man". It must be because her son can now rig elections, I reckon. My immediate younger brother has become the hero of the house.

Papa refused to speak to me even after Mama told him I was still hanging on on the other side. It was Chibuike who told me that Papa was busy with some neighborhood elders who came around to fraternize with them, the winning family of Aladinma Ward 1. I am in the bathroom, brushing my teeth, thinking to myself, so Papa now hosts visitors on Chibuike's behalf.

We are just two of us born to our parents—Chibuike and I. I am the one who ran to Europe because I could no longer stand to watch visitors who came to our house from overseas speak English as if it was not the same language we had always known. I was the one who got angry, easily, because my aunt who stays in Germany said education in Nigeria was trash. I was the one who wanted to send Mama red apples and chocolates, the one who wanted to stop her from asking the visitors, "What did you bring back from America?" I was the one who felt studying Architecture in Nigeria was a waste of Papa's hard-earned spare automobile parts money.

I was the one who felt Chibuike was fucked up when he boldly told me, in the bedroom we shared, "One day, I will rule this useless Imo State, and steal the remaining money. After emptying the state account, I will sell the damn state to the *kora*, the Lebanese people, and run away. Maka chukwu!"

Maybe it's time to return home before Chibuike sells the ward. I may just be there on time to take my share of the sales. I get to Victoria Station, pay twenty-four pounds for a train to Coventry. Today, I will boldly meet Charlie and tell him of my plans. I will tell him that my time to enjoy Naira has come. I will tell him of my plans to drop out of the Ph.D. course and head home where Chibuike has reserved a contract for me through his friends at the State Government House.

"They're here," Charlie yells the moment his eyes meet mine at the station in Coventry. "The silly boys are here."

"What are you talking ab--"

"Sally's useless sons," he says, and he inhales a huge volume of air into his lungs. He now looks like Incredible Hulk.

"They're back to claim the dead woman after all my sufferings. After they made me service that old woman's private part and place my tongue on those weak nipples. And do dishes and all the laundry. Those dirty underwear!"

"But it all doesn't count, son," I hold him by his arms and shake him real hard. And I'm thinking, did I just call him that–son!

"It all doesn't count. They can't lay claim to what belongs to you. It's all written and signed."

Charlie yells in Igbo language. He then yells in English, not the same English Sally had taught him. He slumps and falls upon a bench. His eyes turn red.

I don't know what to say to my friend of ten years. We have known each other before we left Nigeria for the United Kingdom. We were in the same university, Imo State University. Charlie had just gained admission to read Medicine and Surgery when we met at the Registrar's Office. He was a young boy with hopes of better things ahead. He told me all his plans the moment we met.

"I will not stay in all those cheap hostels where you see only village girls. I will go straight to Old English and buy good quality stock jeans and tops. Who wan fall hand for IMSU?"

"I go belong nah. I'll be so rugged, they'll fear me in this school."

"There are freshmen parties everywhere but, I'll never miss that one before matriculation, the one in the night where boys will be made men."

Charlie soon got tired of everything in school, and mostly because he feared he would lose his life. But he acted like my life was more important than his the night we slept in the bush behind Lake Nwebere because there was war in school, and most of our boys were already dead.

"You're still young, Ike," he whispered into my ears. "You're not even in your second year. You can start all over again in Europe. Don't let these boys end the beginning of what could be an enjoyable life for you."

I nodded in acceptance and we slept close to the banks of the lake. Six months later, I convinced Papa to send me to London where I would try again to bring pride back to our house. But I did not tell Papa that I had not had peace since Charlie left Nigeria a couple of months before. He would not let me be with his long calls that stayed hours and made my ears itch. It made me wonder why he needed to waste that much airtime to speak to me just to, through constant echoes, educate me on how very much behind Nigeria was when compared to London city. He harped on how their internet was as swift as light, and how he desired for us to have Skype conversations but could not because of the snail speed of the internet in Nigeria.

* * * * *

Charlie stands up from the bench. He now wants to talk to me. He wants to hug me. He embraces me the same way he did the day we were both initiated into the cult, before he whispered those faint words into my ears—*We are now men*.

But this time he has something different to say, something that makes his eyes wet and his lips quiver. He rests his arms on my shoulders, and looks into my eyes before he lowers his face. There is silence. I do not say a word because I am dazed to see Charlie this way.

"Fuck! Sally was about to write that will before death came calling."

THINGS WE DON'T KNOW

࿔

A na liked troubling those rose petals in front of the house. She would find her way out of the house during forty winks, smell them petal by petal, feel their red suede before plucking them, and giggle while every branch shook at every tug. The bees would fly and buzz about her head, and she would bend and roll from chest to back on the finely mowed green lawn. On the lawn, she would play with grasshoppers and bugs, taking dives at them. That was Ana, a friend to insects and flowers, a listener to nature.

The past few days, she was no more able to leave our bedroom because she was sick with flu and stomach ache. Aunty Clara had, the previous day, gone to a city center chemist shop to ask what drugs were right for her. I had gone with Aunty Clara to meet the chemist. It was a small shop with wooden shelves and countertop in front, where a lady rested her elbow and was fast asleep, nodding at every unintended fall of her head. There was almost nothing in the shop to sell; just condoms, painkillers, insecticides, and disinfectants. I also spotted some scanty bottles of nasal decongestants and other substances. Aunty Clara was not bothered about what drugs the chemist had. She had already boasted to Uncle Eugene about having a better "doctor" than him.

"Wey your Oga?" Aunty Clara asked the lady at the counter who had jerked at the bellow of my aunt. Her eyeballs were now blood surged and it took a few seconds before she responded.

"Oga?" she asked Aunty Clara, stretching her hands above

her head. It made some click sounds.

"Yes, your Oga," Aunty Clara said. "Where is he? I need some prescriptions. My daughter is sick. Two days now. I need to see him."

"Okay," she replied and looked for something behind the counter. When she brought it out, I noticed it was a blue hat, the kind wore by auxiliary nurses. She was what Uncle Eugene called "Nurse Eliza", meaning a nurse without a license.

"Oh! See him coming in. He go to Mama Nji house. The woman no gree well. Die kwanu, she no gree die. Mtchew!" the nurse mumbled.

Aunty Clara and I turned. I noticed a man wearing a red tee shirt with GOLD CIRCLE CONDOM written so boldly on it that one could read it from afar. He tried severally to cross the road, but the traffic sent him back as soon as he made a few steps closer to the edge. After a few more attempts, he crossed, running like an athlete. Aunty Clara heaved a sigh of relief.

"Has it been long since you came?" the man asked my aunt. He was panting from having had to run across the road. There was a slight slice of hope in my heart as soon as he spoke. His English seemed polished.

"Not really, Max," Aunty Clara replied. "You came back at the right time."

"Thank God I didn't keep you waiting," he said. "I have told you to return to the city, but you said your husband wouldn't hear that."

"Don't even say that near him."

"But he can run his farm from the city. He doesn't need to be there every day tilling the soil with the laborers, throwing seeds in the soil, and covering them again. He doesn't need to be there every day, waiting for the season of harvest."

"Eugene would not let anyone suggest to him how to run his farm," Aunty Clara said and giggled. It was only her mouth that made the giggly sound. Her face still looked very troubled.

"Your daughter?" the man asked, staring me in the eyes.

I blushed.

"Oh, no. She's Eunice's," Aunty Clara replied. She stroked my back. "She has been with us for over a year now. Good girl."

"Yes, I'm sure she is. Eunice was a nice woman," he said. "I was troubled when I heard of her demise. It was difficult to accept."

There was forced silence in the shop. Everyone was mute, including the nurse whose eyes were becoming whiter now. It was the same way everyone mourned Mama at the gravesite; in great silence. We all wore black clothes on the day of the funeral. Some wore traditional attires either made of satin, linen or brocades, well designed that they looked nothing like clothes for mourning. The only thing that made all of us look alike was that we all wore black clothes and wept at different tempos. Mama was the first of all her siblings. She was the *Ada*. Aunty Clara was the second.

* * * * *

"Annabelle wants to kill me," Aunty Clara started. "I'm sure she must have sucked too much nectar from the flowers. You know she likes flowers, just like her father. Recently, she keeps crying and complaining of stomach ache, even this morning. And she is also feverish. Everyone is worried. "

"Oh sorry, my dear," Max said. "I understand your situation. It may just be typhoid fever, sometimes it comes with tummy troubles. I'll give you an analgesic to reduce the fever and something for the stomach ache at once. You have to bring her here for proper testing and diagnosis though."

"Okay, doctor. I'll bring her later this evening, once the fever has gone down and the stomach ache too," Aunty Clara promised.

"I understand. Please have a seat. Let me have Nurse Ekwi sort the drugs out for you," he said and turned to me.

"Nne, were oche. Onweghi ihe ga-eme nwanne gi.

* * * * *

Nurse Ekwi, the Eliza nurse, mixed all the drugs the chemist had asked her to in one steel saucer before pouring them inside the transparent sachet. It looked like a concoction. It was a mix of various colors—blue, red, yellow, and white. The chemist then wrote the dosage on a piece of paper and gave it to Aunty Clara.

"After these, I'm sure everything will be fine. But she has to beware of what she eats. Don't let her miss any drug. And she should also drink enough water. It helps in clearing the system."

"Thank you," Aunty Clara said to the man. "I knew I could count on you. I told my husband I could."

The chemist laughed aloud.

We left after my aunt had a few more chats with him. We were readily on the bus back home when Aunty Clara's phone rang three times before she could find it in her big handbag. She surveyed the buttons properly before selecting the right key to punch. She quickly punched another key afterward to make it louder, loud enough to overcome the hindering noise on the bus.

It was bad news.

"Annabelle has left us," Uncle Eugene cried out aloud. "It was appendicitis, and it ruptured in her belly before I was able to drive her to St. Jude's."

THINGS OF THE LORD

Nduka is a good man, dark and handsome. That's what Aunty Julie keeps saying. And all the women who are members of the Mary Sumner group say the same. But the men who belong to the Parochial Church Committee think the women are spellbound by Nduka and are fantasizing. They also say he is the church worker who goes to gossip all the hidden things to the parish priest. The parish priest loves Nduka, just like the women of Mary Sumner, and that is why he took Nduka from Amakohia, where he learned to tap palm wine from his poor father and brought him to St. Stephen's Anglican Church to learn the ways of the Lord.

Nduka came to the famous St. Stephen's as a teenager, with a Ghana-Must-Go bag and a smile that endeared the difficult congregation. And everyone called Nduka whenever they needed anything done in the church. Mothers sent their children to learn from him, while the teenage girls went to visit him at the church vicarage with plastic and stainless steel food flasks. Nduka has worked at the parish for a little under five years and has grown taller and fatter, and now teaches the youth during Sunday School.

In recent times, Nduka has sat before many panels of the Parochial Church Committee for the many things they say he did. Lady Ada accused Nduka of touching her teenage daughter's new breasts, which made the little girl cry all night and had a fever. Sir Ben said Nduka had used his fine and seductive voice to convince his undergraduate daughter to cook and take food to him each morning. And the reports of the many fights that kept happening at the Girls' Guild meetings over who had Nduka's attention the most filled the air in the church.

Venerable Chris would always walk into these panels, holding Nduka by the hand. The young man would stand before the church committee to wash his hands off all the accusations, and the parents would lower their heads in shame. This is why Nduka is no more loved by the many people who once worshipped the ground that he walked on. Nevertheless, he is still loved by a few, like Aunty Julie and some of the women of the Mary Sumner group.

"He will soon be ordained a priest," Aunty Julie says to Isioma. "And he'll return to work under Venerable Chris. He's a young man. We need young people to lead the parish."

"Yes, Aunty," Isioma replies. "The old men will not want him to return. We are having a lot of problems already because of his presence in the church."

"He is not the reason for all the problems," Aunty Julie cuts in. She attempts to lift the coal-stained pot from the big kerosene stove. Isioma rushes ahead of her, picks up the rags on the floor next to the stove, wraps them around her two palms, and lifts the pot by the handles. She feels the heat as she wrinkles her face.

"Drop it here on that table," Aunty Julie says as she clears the wooden table that is next to the sink.

"When is he leaving?" Isioma asks Aunty Julie after she drops the pot of Oha soup and opens the lid halfway to allow the steam and aroma escape into the hot air of the kitchen.

"Who?" Aunty Julie asks.

"Nduka," Isioma reminds her. "You said he's leaving for the

School of Theology soon. I am wondering when."

"I don't know about that yet," Aunty Julie says. "I only know Venerable Chris has gotten the approval of the Bishop to include him as soon as he meets all requirements."

Both women, in their mid-fifties and twenties respectively, sit down on the kitchen stools to talk about many other things that have to do with the parish, the Parochial Church Committee, the Anglican Youth Fellowship, EFAC and the Scripture Union, and also the women of Mary Sumner.

Aunty Julie is called *Aunty Julie* by everyone in the church, including the older congregation. She is called so because no one knows any of her relatives as no one ever visits her. She has no husband and no children. She lives in Egbu Housing Estate, in a small low-income flat building that scarcely had external set-backs. But she uses her small backyard as a garden for pumpkins, water leaves, scent leaves and a few other vegetables. Egbu Housing Estate is an estate for the young and the old. There are little boys and girls in the streets, chatting and giggling, and admiring their newly formed body organs. They are playing football at the school grass field, smoking cigarettes, and having new girlfriends. The streets are full of life.

A couple at Road 8 fight and shout every morning and no one is ever able to figure out who is the victim amongst both of them. They walk out of their premises, always, with joy written on their faces. There is also the house where all the boys take the girls to. And this is the same house where poker cards are played and fights happen every day. The neighborhood people keep meeting and discussing how to use the vigilante to stop them from smoking marijuana and letting the entire estate smell of it.

Aunty Julie's house remains silent, and people fear she may one day die and decompose without anyone getting to know about it.

* * * * *

It is Palm Sunday, and everyone is raising palm branches and leaves, and singing *Hallelujah* songs in remembrance and celebration of Jesus Christ. Venerable Chris is leading the procession while Nduka is behind him. The choristers of St. Stephen's Anglican Church are behind Nduka, singing aloud and dancing. There is a lot of rambling gossips in the crowd. A day before, Nduka did what no one has ever done in the state. He went to the heart of the city, found an illicit refuse dump in the middle of the major road, stepped into the rubbles and climbed all the way to the top. He stood at the top of the dump and sang so many religious songs, and then he gave a loud sermon that filtered into the air of the popular market, right before the press took interest in his actions. The city of Owerri went agog. And those who recognized him said he had gone mad and needed some care. Even this morning, as the congregation of St. Stephen's Anglican Church parade the streets of Owerri, most of the members are saying he has gone insane.

"He was only being audible for the Lord Jesus, rebuking all the evil traders," Venerable Chris explained before the congregation left for the procession. But it was already too late for the members of the Parochial Church Committee to believe the defense by the priest.

At the end of the service, no one is seen near Nduka. No one sends their children to him to help him pack all the leaves and tidy up the altar. He is left alone to tidy up the entire church after

60

a busy Sunday. He paces about from the altar to the choir pews, and then the church hall, sweeping and humming some hymnals, the ones that the choir sang earlier in the day. After a couple of hours, he is done and he slumps on the floor of the altar. He sleeps off, and his snores are replied by the echoes that come from the walls of St. Stephen's Anglican Church.

In the morning, Aunty Julie cooks and thinks about Nduka. She is the only one who remembers him after the news of his insanity traveled around the city. She stuffs huge volume of spiced grains of jollof rice into a big green food flask, seals it with the lid and hands it over to Isioma who carefully secures it in a big nylon bag. Aunty Julie rubs off the oil on her hands on her skirt.

"Make sure he eats it this morning," Aunty Julie says. "I'm sure he hasn't had any decent meal since those Mary Sumner witches abandoned him."

"But, Aunty," Isioma says in a low voice, like one who has a secret to tell. "Is he really mad?"

"Tufiakwa! Chukwu ekwekwana," Aunty Julie hushes her. "God forbid. He's not."

"Why did he leave the comfort of the vicarage to preach at the refuse dump?" Isioma asks.

"I don't know, Nwam," Aunty Julie answers. "Just take the food to him. You can ask him why he did that when you get there. But be smart, so you can return to your mother as fast as possible. They're already telling her not to let you come to this house anymore."

"Who?" Isioma asks. "Who told you that?"

"Your mother told me," Aunty Julie replies. "She is a good

woman with a pure heart. She will not let the witches spoil her. No, she will not."

Isioma walks into the church hall and the little boys of the Boys Brigade are already sounding their drums and trumpets in what seems like a rehearsal. It is a holiday period and the priest has created a program for the youths. The boys are to rehearse with the Brigade band, while the girls are to learn to bake cakes. The entire premise is noisy, and some boys are romping about the church hall, causing more chaos. To Isioma, it is a dump site for parents who don't want their children at home during the holidays. They conveniently drop them at the church, under nobody's supervision. Isioma turns around to see if she can catch a glimpse of Nduka. She doesn't seem to notice his presence which is always pronounced. Isioma grabs one of the boys running around the church hall.

"Where is Nduka?" she asks. "Where can I find him?"

The little dark boy giggles and hides behind Isioma, like he is hiding from his playmates.

"Aunty, I haven't seen him this morning," he says while panting. He chuckles even more.

"He hasn't been to the church this morning?" Isioma asks him.

"I don't know, Aunty," he says and eases his hands out of Isioma's grab. "And my mother warned me not to get close to him. She said Uncle Nduka is mad."

He runs off again, back to his peers, and they are giggling and running all around the church hall and into the spaces between the pews. The noise in the church, of little children and many drums and trumpets, grows even louder that Isioma veils her right ear with her hand and holds the nylon sack in her left hand. She walks through the church and into the vestry, and finds her way out and at the back of the church where she meets some quiet and sanity.

Isioma has never been to Nduka's room. But because she needs to drop food with him and return Aunty Julie's flask as soon as possible, she is in front of his door knocking and hoping to be let in. She knocks on the door for a while, and then the knock gradually grows louder and becomes a bang. The door caves in, and there stands Nduka before Isioma, with skin as smooth and fine as the desert sand, and hairs that stand on his hands like a crowd of humans in the worship of a god. Nduka is a handsome young man. He is the secret wish of the young girls of the choir. Even mothers had joined with their daughters to desire Nduka before he was rumored to have gone insane. Isioma searches for the right words to erupt from her mouth. Her lips seem locked, and the more she tries, the more it seems like they have been bonded by an adhesive.

"Aunty Julie called me on the phone," Nduka says. "She said you were coming with food."

"Yes," Isioma replies. Her head is lowered to the ground, and she forces her eyes down as well anytime they meet with Nduka's bold black eyes. "She said you should..."

"I have a small pot to turn the food in," Nduka steals the words out of Isioma's lips. He slides his fingers into the handle of Isioma's nylon bag and Isioma lets go of the bag. Their hands brush against each other. Nduka smiles. Isioma keeps her head lowered, and her knees bob as though held by loose springs.

"Come in," Nduka screams from inside. "I need to get the

pot washed. It will take a minute or two. Come inside. The mosquitoes these days have gone angrier. Come in and shut the door."

Isioma steps into Nduka's bedroom, which is a self-contained one bedroom, large enough that Nduka's bags and clothes, and every other thing, are at only a corner of the bedroom while there is much more unused space. Isioma leans on the wall by the entrance door. Nduka is not the only one in his bedroom that morning. Isioma responds to the greeting of a boy in his teens, sitting on Nduka's bed and watching *WrestleMania* which is showing on the 14" television screen. He looks familiar to Isioma, but she waves off the burden of thinking out whom his parents are. There is beauty in his smiles and the way he gets off the bed anytime Stone Cold Steve Austin punches his weary and unfortunate opponent in the face, or anytime he lifts him up and slams him against the floor of the wrestling ring. The boy laughs and claps at all the things he is seeing on the television. Isioma starts smiling too. She is fascinated by the teenager's love for the sport.

"Please, send my greetings to Aunty Julie," Nduka returns the flask to Isioma. "Tell her that I am grateful for all her kindness towards me. She is my guardian angel."

"Sure, I will," Isioma assures Nduka. She collects the nylon bag from him. It is lighter now. She flings it about in a semi-circular vacillation.

"You are always welcome, Isioma," Nduka says. This time, the words seem like they forcefully broke through the bars of his lips, like some lucky prisoners. "You can always come to the vicarage. You can visit me anytime."

"Okay," Isioma replies him. She does not say another word. Her head lowers to the ground again. And she softly touches the handle of the door and opens it. The air of the open filled Nduka's bedroom. Isioma walks outside and takes her steps, one at a time, out of Nduka's sight and out of the vicarage. She walks to the front of the west door of the church. She stops, takes a deep breath and her breasts bloat and then falls flat again. Isioma shuts her eyes, smiles and lets the August breeze brush against her chubby cheeks.

* * * * *

On the last Sunday in August, everyone is screaming in church immediately after the benediction, and chatting in very many small groups. The band members are gathered around the drums, while the choristers are close to the vestry. St. John's Family are gathered at the East door, while St. Matthias' Family are together at the western entrance. The church knights and church committee are with the vicar, very close to the altar. Everywhere, in echoes, Nduka's name is heard quite audibly oozing from the mouths of the entire congregation. Heads are shaking in disapproval, even Venerable Chris' head. After a few minutes, the women regroup and gather together again, now as Mary Sumner women. Aunty Julie joins them. She rests her hands on her head and lets out a scream. No one turns to stare at her. All the other women are screaming too. Lady Ijenwanyi rushes into the church hall and makes her way to the altar where she falls at the feet of Venerable Chris. Her husband, a tall man of good flesh, runs after her and tries to pick her up. Venerable Chris holds him and stops him.

Isioma is standing on the aisle and watching, drops of tears running down her cheeks. She wraps her arms around her breasts and quivers as if she is cold. She is watching the entire sad drama. She is feeling like she let it happen. She blames herself, but she tells no one. She tells no one that she was there, yesterday, at Nduka's bedroom. She tells no one that she saw Kaeside in Nduka's bedroom, happy and laughing off at the wrestling match showing on the television. She tells no one that she stood there and watched WrestleMania with Kaeside and never knew his name until everyone started calling him that this morning.

She tells no one that although he wore only shorts in Nduka's bedroom, she never thought it was absurd enough to attract thoughts of abnormality. She is never going to tell anyone that she was there, that morning, and gave Nduka food. She thinks he must have been energized and recovered after eating the food. She is never going to tell anyone that she walked away, yesterday, leaving behind the smokes and stench of marijuana in Nduka's bedroom.

THINGS OF THE DARK

S cratch hardly drinks alcohol. He only stands behind the turntable and amplifiers and nods his head in approval to all the songs he is playing. He hardly even dances while everyone at Club 202 is dancing and chatting and drinking, and the guys with their girlfriends have their loins pinned to the buttocks of these girls of the night, following in rhythm to the sound of the music and movements of the buttocks. One hardly sees him at his usual spot—the DJ spot—except for the few times the disco spotlights would flash and fall on his face. Many clubbers do not know Scratch by the day, when the sun is out and people are in the streets, going about their daily businesses.

Scratch perfectly mixes up with passersby and pedestrians without being noticed, except by a few who know him too well. But everyone knows Scratch by the fluency in the way he slides from one hit track to another, making it seem like a progression of the same sound; and also how he goes up-tempo when people are high on alcohol and can virtually dance to just about any sound. Some club nights, Scratch would witness the celebrity experience as some of the girls would try to run up to the DJ stand, but the well-built bodyguards on black tee shirts would hold them back with their large arms.

It is another night and exactly 1 a.m. Scratch has just climbed up the DJ stand and announced his name through the hype man who was also in the dark corner and unseen. He starts off with Bob Marley's *Stir it Up*, and all the clubbers are screaming and hopping one step after the other in rhythm to the song.

Richard is a waiter. The club manager insists he works at the club on Fridays. He is assigned to coordinate the other waiters because of his muscular build and the correctness of his spoken English. He is also assigned to serve the very important personalities with the sign *VIP* tagged on the beam leading to a much darker corner of the nightclub. Richard is the image of Club 202, the very tall and fit young man, fair in complexion and well-spoken in his adopted Queen's English. He is the one the very rich clubbers know, the one the ladies slide torn papers with telephone numbers into his pocket so he can help pass them to the rich boys in the VIP. He is the one the ladies smile to, the one who has been able to match rich boys with hustling girls.

And although Richard is priced with sex, a few times, he remains decent and faithful to his relationship with his undergraduate lover. After each club night, he clears the VIP of empty bottles, cigarette butts, and champagne glasses, changes back to mufti and in a neighbor's *Keke Napep*, heads straight to his apartment. The *keke* driver is the same neighbor who works late at night taking night clubbers to their very many places.

Tonight, with smiles on his face, Richard is ushering Obodo and two of his friends into the VIP corner. Obodo is smiling too. They are with three girls who are now dancing to Bob Marley's *Stir it up* played by Scratch who is beautifully interrupted by the hype man announcing Obodo's entrance into Club 202. Obodo eases some naira notes into Richard's hands and points at the hype man. And Richard heads to the hype man to give him the money.

* * * * *

"*Oya*, you girls should hurry up," Zubby says to the scarcely clad girls who work as the strippers for the VIP and VVIP guests. "Big boys don dey vex. We need to make them happy."

"No wahala," replies Nina, a slim, pretty face and dark girl with small breasts. Her voice sounds as small as her breasts. "We are set *na*. Just I and the two others are okay for the VIP. We are set to go with you. Abi, girls no be so?"

"Na so na," chorus the two other girls, Ije and Amaka.

"Ngwanu, make we match dey go," Zubby says and walks out of the female changing room while the three ladies, dressed in only underwear, follow after him. Zubby is Club 202's pimp, regularly contracted to bring in female strippers on club nights for the very rich guests. He has been so steady and reliable that the manager has completely left him to sort that aspect of the club all by himself. He has come to settle with a few of his regular ladies that are always available, loyal, and understand what the rich guests of Club 202 love. And although he influences his girls to make the guests happy, he maintains his golden rules—*no touch customer blokos, no kiss customer,* and *no collect business cards*. If a customer needs extra services, outside the regulars provided by the strippers, he is to meet with Zubby who collects some fees for those services.

* * * * *

Scratch infuses *Naija* genre of music—from Tuface to D'Banj, Wizkid, and Davido, and Kiss Daniel, and the already high-spirited crowd on the dance floors are screaming and dancing around in different kinds of dance. Cigarette fumes grace the heads and faces of people, and some corners are entirely blinded by billows from *shisha* pipes. The only thing everyone shares is the trending music Scratch plays and the happiness that permeates the entire space. Club 202 is lit again tonight.

1:00am

"Richie," Obodo calls aloud. "Abeg come make we yarn."

"Boss," Richard answers and drops a new set of Moet and Chandon Champagne, with sparks from disco lights tied to the six bottles, on the glass table before Obodo and his friends. He moves closer to Obodo, his ear close to Obodo's mouth.

"How e go be na?" Obodo says. His screams reduce a little. But he struggles to be audible amongst the banging audio speakers which stand close to him. "How will you make it happen? I'm tripping, my guy!"

"Boss, I don't get," Richard replies. "What do you want me to make happen? I won't waste time on it."

"Correct guy," Obodo hollers. He giggles a bit and nods his head. "I'm tripping for this girl, the one dancing and climbing the pole. *Nwa agbakala m isi.* I cannot think of anything anymore."

"Nina?" Richard queries. He leads Obodo to her direction with his forefinger.

"Yes, she is the one," Obodo answers. "I need her before she starts pulling off those panties for everyone to see what Obodo wants to chop."

Both young men giggle aloud, their shoulders quaking as if they are epileptic. Obodo used to be the street boy that mingled with older boys in the neighborhood where Richard grew up with his cousins and aunt. Although dark in complexion with tribal marks which make him look like an aborigine from Benin,

Obodo has always been this Igbo boy that was growing up in Nkwere before the bitter spice of sadness dropped into the pot of his life. He came to live in Owerri as a houseboy to one of the rich people in the estate. But Obodo soon ran away and became a street boy, running errands, buying cigarettes and marijuana for the bad boys. He became popular amongst teenagers and notorious to parents. Everyone said he joined the bad gang and grew with them. Some say he is now a *Yahoo Boy*. But to Richard, Obodo remains a young man who has hustled in the streets, doing everything a wild African boy does to survive. Now that he has become rich and even good-looking, no one must count his past against him. Even the tribal marks do not count now.

"Nina is Zubby's girl," Richard says to Obodo. "Zubby is the one who holds the knife."

"I know Zubby is the pimp," Obodo replies.

"No," Richard hushes him. "Nina is much more than his product. She is his woman. His babe."

"You don't mean it."

"I'm for real, Boss," Richard continues. "A few people have tried taking Nina out of this place. But Zubby never agrees. He fumes a lot anytime someone makes an offer for her."

"Oh, really?" Obodo says. He exhales and leans on the dark wall. The random disco lights fall on him, and darts of *blue-green-yellow-pink* lights spot all over his body like he has become a target in a shooting game. His very expensive body-hug button white shirt is revealed. Scratch switches to Sugarboy's *Holla* and Obodo nods to the rhythm.

"You know what?" Richard says, looking like he has just made a discovery. "Let me have your business card. I'll find a way to slip it into her bra or something. It's a win or lose thing. She may call you tomorrow morning."

"Now, that's a great idea," Obodo praises Richard. "Let me get you one from my wallet."

He brings out his leather wallet from his back pocket and takes out a card. He shields it from any prying eyes and carefully slides it into Richard's breast pocket like he was bribing a highway mobile police officer.

"No *wahala*," Richards assures Obodo. And he walks away from the VIP, briskly, not looking back.

2:30am

Zubby is screaming in the female changing room. All the girls in the room are quiet. He is the only one screaming in English and Igbo languages. No one says anything to him. They also say nothing to one another. Everything in the room is still, even the air. No breathing for fear it may interrupt and irritate him and get him even angrier. So no pin drops. Zubby is the only creature pacing about the entire space and screaming. And then he stops.

"She walked out of the VIP before we could notice," Amaka finally responds to Zubby's queries in her soft and tender tone that made it look like she was saying her last words. "We thought you called her out."

"Yes, I too felt you were the one who called Nina out of the VIP," Ije says, supporting Amaka. Both young girls nod.

"I didn't call her," Zubby says. He slumps and sits on a soft stool by the dressing mirror. "I never even noticed when she left. Nina has followed another man tonight. I know it."

"You cannot be too sure, Zubby," Ije says. "She may have stepped out to smoke or something."

"Or she may just not be okay where she is," Amaka responds.

"She is well," Zubby assures her. "I know Nina. She must have followed another rich dude for the cash. I know how desperate she has become lately."

Zubby lowers his head and places his hands on it, and shakes it in disapproval.

"I must find her," Zubby starts screaming again. "I am Zubby. *Na me*! There is nothing I cannot find. She is coming back to me tonight. Nina thinks I am a baby. She will confirm tonight that I am the Don."

* * * * *

Zubby stands from the stool and kicks it. It falls and rolls under the dresser. Ije and Amaka jolt and move away. He dashes out of the room and slams the door against the girls. And the room returns to silence. No one says a word again.

2:45am

Nina is quite pretty and on a scale of ten over ten when it comes to Obodo's ratings. He tells her this as she drops her small handbag on the side table and eases off her shoes close to the reading table in his hotel room. She then pulls off her bra and trousers and hangs them on a hook by the wardrobe door. She enters the bathroom. Obodo knows she has gone to have a quick bath, to shower off all the sweats of her hustle up and down the dancing pole in the VIP corner of Club 202. He knows he will join her soon, but he paces happily about the bedroom space, a newscaster on CNN talking about things Obodo is not interested in. He waits a little. He waits for all fantasies to set in. He waits for Nina to be completely naked and wet in the shower. He waits for the right time to see her beautiful hourglass-shaped body, to hold and own it. The time is finally here, and Obodo gently pushes down the door handle and tiptoes into the bathroom.

There is a pool of blood all around Nina's body. It is her blood. And she is lying face-up on the floor tiles, unmoving and not saying a word. The waters from the shower sprinkle on her breasts and face and thighs and wash off her blood through the drains. There is hot steam in the bathroom that completely veils the dressing mirror hung on the wall close to the water closet. And although the air is hot, Obodo knows that Nina has gone cold, and will never answer to all his calls and jabs and that the beginning of his new troubles has come. He knows he is to think fast. He is to either call the paramedic or elope from the hotel. He is to think fast and overcome his fears. And although he signs into the hotel, regularly, with a name that does not belong to him – *Peter Cockwell,* he knows he is famous and everyone knows Obodo, even the hotel staff whom he tips anytime he is in the lobby.

* * * * *

Scratch is out of the stand. He has handed over to his intern, a boy on dreads that is as light as the morning sun, and which shines even brighter when disco lights fall on his fine face. The diminishing crowd at Club 202 screams aloud as he plays *Fall on You* by Davido. Scratch is now on the dance floor, dancing and drinking with anyone who cares to have him. He does not dance with any girl for long before he smiles and leaves for another. It is his game. He knows he is never to pay interest in any particular girl at the club. He knows girls are generally jealous, and it may cost him his popularity. So Scratch moves on and on, from the dark corner of the *Popular Stand* to the long aisle where the sex traders line up resting their arms on the galvanized railings and showing off their well-shaped backs as selling points.

Scratch has the talisman, for as he dances and moves and greets, everyone tries to dance along and exchange pleasantries, which masks huge appreciations over the happy mood on which he has set every corner of Club 202. He continues dancing and walking around until he is brought to a stop when his right arms clashes against someone and the hot wetness and stench of whiskey is felt and perceived by Scratch. He raises his arm and examines carefully like a scientist would in the laboratory at a new organism in a test tube. Someone has poured some whiskey on his arm. And that someone is now clenching him by the left hand and showing remorsefulness over the obvious excitement and happy moments that caused the spill.

She is the beautiful lady, Dabota, the Port Harcourt born new accountant with a new multinational haulage company. She is the loner everyone seems to be talking about. She lives in a little apartment, three poles away from City Sky Hotel, the same estate which hosts Club 202. Scratch raises his face, their eyes meet, and what seems like many muted but loud and soft words escape out of his eyes. Dabota lowers her face, smiles, and acceptance ooze through the sweet aroma of her perfume and the smell of cigarette which she leaves on the ashtray to burn away as she allows Scratch to cloth all of her with the gaze of his eyes.

3:15am

At the small space, which is the lobby of City Sky Hotel, Obodo is on the terrazzo floor, wriggling like an earthworm touched by a pinch of salt. He is screaming and yammering all sorts of words and names that everyone in the hotel lobby is aware of. But the most dominant name that left his helpless breath is Nina whom he has left in the shower with the fountain of water sprinkling from the shower head, draining every drop of blood through the floor drains. The hotel security, two men dressed in sky blue shirts and dark trousers, run up the flight of stairs as he mentions Nina even more and points upwards. As Obodo continues to yell, the duty manager holds him to the ground for him not to wriggle more. The front desk staff is on the phone with someone she is shouting at and throwing her left hand in the air as if she speaks through the same hand.

Before this night, Obodo was a regular at the hotel. He has been keeping a room permanently for himself, which he paid for at the end of each month. Although he does not always sleep in the deluxe space, furnished like it was meant for a royal blood, Obodo always makes sure no one gets the opportunity to use the only posh bedroom called "Royalty Suite" for the over thirteen months since the news of his intimidating wealth spread across the city. He would tip the hotel staff a lot of cash, from the gate to room service, especially on weekends because they were his most happy days.

Every receptionist at City Sky Hotel prayed to be on duty when Obodo arrived each weekend to check into Royalty Suite. And on his checkout days, at the end of the weekend, he would also leave some wads of naira notes with the early morning staff, especially the housekeepers, and he would explain that they were the last notes in his possession. A few times, during week-days, Obodo would call the hotel to let Okanu, his closest friend, use his room because he said it was not yet Okanu's turn to make his own huge money. However, he said Okanu's time would defi-nitely come, and he would be able to pay for such luxury.

Okanu, the young boy with a huge chest and large arms, rushes into the lobby of City Sky Hotel. He stands in the middle, on the same Arabian carpet that Obodo is now kneeling on. He hastily surveys with his eyes as he pants and finds air, his chest threatening to pull off buttons from his multi-colored shirt. He throws his eyes on everyone at the lobby, including the hotel security men that are standing next to Obodo.

"No be me, *Nwanne*," Obodo manages to say his first clear words. "I didn't touch her. I haven't even touched her yet. She asked to have a shower. I showed her the bathroom. And that was it. She went in there and died."

"*Gini?*" Okanu asks. "Who died? *Onye?*"

"Nina," Obodo is yapping again. "The girl at the club."

"The girl at the club? The-the-the stripper?" Okanu stutters.

"Yes. The stripper. The one I left with," Obodo confirms. "*Onwuola!*"

"What?"

"Yes! She's there. She is on the bathroom floor, lying like cooked vegetables. She did not open her eyes. She never even tried to look at me. Blood everywhere, Okanu. Blood! I did not do it. Believe me. I did not."

Okanu folds his arms and paces about the lobby. He walks to

the counter and slaps the countertop. A loud sound erupts and echoes on the walls of the lobby. He slaps again, again and again. He stops and everyone is quiet.

"Has anyone called the police?" Okanu asks, in a low tone, as if he is asking himself.

"Yes, we have," the duty manager says.

Obodo raises his face and there is fire in his eyes. He pants like a horse that is thirsty after a big chase. Then everyone at the lobby turns to stare at the duty manager who is stammering some meaningless words, trying to explain the reason for his action.

3:30am

Three armed police officers rush into the hotel lobby. They are wearing navy blue bulletproof vests with POLICE noticeably written on them. But Scratch and Dabota are already standing at the lobby with Obodo and Okanu as the police officers walk into the hotel.

"Where is the criminal?" bellows the police officer in a baritone. He engages his AK47 and the sound forced everyone to cringe. "*Where dem dey?*"

"Officer," says Okanu. "No be criminal. Na fall the girl fall. She must have slipped in the shower."

"Shut up!" yells the police officer. And the other police officers also engage their guns. "Where the body dey?"

"She's on the floor," replies the security officer. "She don cold. Nothing in her is alive."

Obodo slumps to the ground again and starts yelling. He yells so loud that other guests of the hotel begin to gather at the lobby, some in their pajamas and underwear. They query anyone they meet in the lobby. But everyone remains unflinchingly unresponsive.

"You must be Obodo," said the police officer who introduces himself as Inspector Ike. He then orders his men to go confirm the incident.

They run off at once like someone had just blown a whistle and started off a race. And it is not long before they return, nodding their heads in disapproval. They whisper words into Inspector Ike's ears. The whispering lasts for a long time. And when they are done, they cuff Obodo's wrists to the back, drag him up and push him into the trunk of the navy blue truck that is parked outside the premises of the hotel. They say Nina was killed, shot in the head with a gun.

Obodo hears all this, and even more. At the station, he is asked to sit behind the counter. *It seems he strangled her before he pulled the trigger to ensure she was dead and gone,* says one of the officers that returned with them. And then he assures Obodo that it is going to be a very long night for all of them at the police station.

WATER AND THE THINGS
THAT SEPARATE US

༄

Johnson woke up to the sound of a speedboat that anchored at his seaside backyard of Povita, Badagry. It was not the first of such a sound that he always heard from travelers, researchers, tourists, and sometimes, fishermen. But of all his fifteen years of relocating to the border town for his research on *AQUATIC SPECIES OF BADAGRY,* Johnson was yet to have a boat berth in his backyard by midnight. He stood from his five feet mattress which he kept on the floor on top of a raffia mat by the timber louvered window. He lit his lantern with a matchstick, and he tried to unhinge the window to catch a glimpse. There was a gunshot at his backyard. And Johnson laid flat on the cold mud floor. He knew it was not the local fireworks that the youths of Povita occasionally fired because it was Christmas. He knew it was a hunter's gun because it also did not sound like the guns fired by the police when they came to rescue him from the decoy of the angry natives. Johnson turned off his kerosene lantern and remained in his position; he kissed the floor and breathed the dust thereof.

After the gunshot, there were a few rants by some men who sounded like they were not teenagers but in their mid-lives. And things started hitting the zinc roof of his mud house after one of the men ordered that things be thrown at the house. Johnson could only make out what was thrown on top of his roof when he began to hear the rattling sound of burning roofing sheets and the smell of petroleum that eased its way into his nostrils. He did not do much of thinking before he stood, quickly. Rushing to the sack bag where he threw in all his research papers, photographs, and camera, the fifty-year-old grabbed it by the handle and made his way to the façade of the house. He stopped when he was out, briefly allowed a deep breath, and then he hung the handle of the sack on his shoulder and ran as fast as possible for his life.

In the early hours of the morning, when Johnson returned to his house with the traditional ruler, he could not clearly say where his house was standing before that night's heinous visit. He paced about his premises, his hands on his head. Johnson collapsed his knees to the ground and knelt on the floor. He yelled and hit his palm against the red mud. And he began to curse, from man to woman, and every youth and enemies, and everyone who had hatched evil plans against him. The traditional ruler did not look impressed as he punched the stud of his walking stick into the red mud, opening many potholes in anger. He then walked to the backyard where he stood by the shores and looked deep into the sea as though he knew where the assailants had quickly sailed to after their evil acts. But all in the sea were rippling waters, flying flamingos and strange birds, coconut trees on little islands, a plantation of reed, and fishermen who threw their nets in a distance, oblivious of what had happened in the early hours of the morning.

"Any man that has lived in Badagry for as much as five years is one of us," the traditional ruler said to the villagers at the community town hall where he had them gathered.

"Johnson cannot remain a stranger among us. He has lived with us. He has eaten with us. We cannot continue to threaten his life and the wonderful works he is doing for our community."

No one uttered a word as the traditional ruler spat out his

grievances and fire of annoyance, as he threw his fist in the air, punching every word into the ears of his people. They remained quiet as he started and finished his last sentence, and left the town hall with his cabinet members and Johnson. Then they started mumbling and saying many things. Quite a few thought Johnson meant good for the community by drawing the attention of the government to the riverbanks of Badagry and the lives that exist in their waters. But most of them were sure Johnson had become a government agent, sent to discover the potentials of the town, after which they would send a battalion of soldiers against the people and drive them out of their lands and their waters. They gathered in very many cells and argued Johnson's motives until it was dark again and everyone went back to their homes. Johnson slept in the quarters of the palace and rested his head on the sack bag, the only thing he saved from the spell.

After a couple of weeks, the traditional ruler ordered that a house be raised for Johnson on the same land and that every young man in the village was to help with the construction. And even though the villagers were not impressed by the traditional ruler's decision to rebuild Johnson's house, they all gathered at the site. Johnson, who seemed overjoyed by the news, stood before the crowd of young men and women, and he told them how he wanted the house to be built, every material to be locally sourced from the lands and the waters of Badagry. He was ready to build a *Badagry House*; a house that would breathe the nature of the town.

"He wants to build with the bamboo," said one of the young men who obeyed the order of the traditional ruler that morning. He was one of the very few who had come to work with Johnson from the very first day he arrived in Badagry. He was the young man who helped him with chores and a few distant errands.

"This your master can think from his *bum-bum*," replied Philip who had also joined in the reconstruction when he heard that the traditional ruler had ordered the young women to provide food for the men who were working. He became ecstatic when he heard a meal or two could be served. That morning, he quickly wore his half-gone rubber slippers, mud-stained knickers, and a brown singlet torn at the tummy.

"Don't call him my master, Philip. Do you want Papa to be the one to burn this new house when he hears this master of a thing?"

"But the Igbo man shows huge interest in you, Francis," Philip said with a mischievous demeanor, and then smiles that grew into giggles. He clapped his hands as he made a jest of the relationship between Francis and Johnson, laughing like the women at the market who enjoyed the emptiness of their rivals' shops on good market days.

"*Bad Market*," Badagry women would audibly jest, meaning no customer who visited the market would ever patronize the shops of their enemies.

"Have you ever asked him about his children and, maybe, wife? Does he have any, Francis?"

"I think he does. He just prefers not to talk about them," Francis said. "He talks about Manchester a lot. I think they are abroad."

"That's if he has a family," Philip countered. He then started to whisper as he sighted Johnson approach them. Johnson was not a well-built man. Fair in complexion, he had started allowing the liberty of beards growing on his jaw and cheek. He had little or no time to shave, he had claimed, when Francis had the guts to inquire once.

"I have found a lot of bamboo in the creeks," Johnson sounded quite excited. "What are both of you doing standing there? Let's get our hands soiled. Francis, pick up the two machetes. We are sailing to the creeks to cut some bamboo. They need to be dry and set in a couple of weeks."

Both young men stared at each other before Francis made haste to pick up the two machetes from the wooden worktop Johnson had constructed and set his clamp ready for chopping, smoothening and cutting of timber. He threw one of the machetes to Philip. Philip was careful to grab it by the head, and then quickly ran after Francis who was already making efforts to catch up with Johnson at the anchorage. Johnson lifted the engine of his boat as the young men boarded, and took out all the dirt that had stuck to the blades. He then dropped the engine back into the water and turned to catch a glimpse of Francis and Philip who were seated and smiling at him. Johnson smiled back. He untied the rope that held the boat to a kola tree, pulled it in and allowed it to drop carelessly on the floor of the boat. Francis and Philip gripped the frame of the wooden boat as Johnson started and quickly sailed far away, deep into the ocean.

Before long, they got to a little island with bamboo trees standing majestically like many Sankweto masquerades dancing to the beating of Sato drums of the sea breeze and bowing at the peak of their heights. Johnson switched off the engine and allowed the boat to sail quietly and unaided to the banks of the creek. There, he held the stalk of a dry bamboo and moving with the boat, he pulled himself towards the stem where he tied and knotted the rope he had dropped into the boat earlier before they set sail. He clapped his palms, as though clearing dirty, but all that exuded from his demeanor were the words, "*It is time.*"

"We'll cut as much as our arms can reach," Johnson said. "We are lucky to find as much as we need."

"Oh, yes," Philip said, stood and tried to catch his balance as the boat rocked like a pendulum. "I knew we would find a lot of them. There's hardly much need for them these days."

"No," Johnson bellowed amidst the sound of a rushing wind. "You're wrong. Badagry is lucky to have them. You can find as much as these anywhere near Lagos."

"What do they need them for?" Francis asked.

"A whole lot!" Johnson replied.

"A whole lot?" Philip echoed.

"Yes," Johnson said. "You are lucky to be out here with me. Very many things to learn. And the earlier we start, the better. We do not have much time. The clouds are gathering. It won't be a nice encounter if we were caught in the ocean by the rains."

And Johnson took the machete from Philip. He picked a tiny piece of blue cloth from the floor of the boat and tied it around the head of the machete. Both young men knew it was Johnson's little way of protecting his palms and fingers from blisters. They nodded as he threw his hand and the blade cut through the air and landed deep into the stalk of a bamboo tree, and the boys heard the first sound, like teeth crushing the bones of a fried Christmas chicken.

After they had fallen over a hundred stems of bamboo, Johnson slumped on a bench and asked the young men to join him. Panting like dogs that had just returned from hunting in the wild, Francis, followed by Philip, joined Johnson to sit on the bench facing him. The boat rocked and Johnson shook his head sideways for a moment and stopped, and smiled.

"Badagry is a special place," Johnson said. "This did not start today."

"What did not start today, sir?" Philip asked. Francis smiled and nodded his head.

"The tussle," Francis said to Philip.

"Yes, the tussle," Johnson repeated. "The Egun people are blessed."

Johnson brought out three bowls from under his feet, and then a nylon bag that was robust with something inside. Philip and Francis focused on what he had in his hands. Seemingly surprised to have seen that Johnson had come along with a little bag of garri, cubes of sugar and some water, they heaved a sigh and accepted the bowls which he had shown before them. Johnson poured a few grains into their bowls, threw in a cube of sugar into each bowl before he poured in water and asked them to stir.

"Too much sugar is not good for anyone," Johnson said, and then stirred his bowl to produce a finely mixed meal of cereal, after the cube of sugar had melted like salt under water.

"You said Badagry is special?" Philip recounted Johnson's words, and then stared at him, waiting for him to speak.

"Yes, and a bloody land too," Johnson continued. "The white men started the problems of Agbedagari and instilled the fears that you find in the eyes of the people. I don't blame the people when they find strangers as a threat to their existence. And now, the government. Chasing the Eguns from one waterfront to the other, taking all that rightfully belongs to them."

The young men paid rapt attention to Johnson while their cereal soaked up all the water and became as hard as wet mud. Francis dropped his bowl on the floor of the boat and Philip did the same. Johnson's voice became a bit more nourished and grew louder that they echoed on the waters. He then said many things about how the people were losing their fishermen, and no one was really interested in commercial farming. Although he never said it, the boys knew he was getting annoyed by the wrinkles that had formed on his face and the way his voice fluctuated like the sound of an old 911 heavy truck on a potholed road. Johnson said that this was not the dream of Agbedeh, the famous farmer who tilled all the lands. He blamed the Portuguese slave merchant, George Freemingo, for opening the eyes of the people to quick money made through slave trade around the 1660s.

"Thank God the last ship left for Brazil already," Johnson said. "I would have remained in my Enugu. But young men are returning to fishing now and farming. This is the only way out."

"How will it bring back the trust?" Philip asked.

"Oh! The trust?" Johnson repeated. "That one na gorment wahala. Anytime dem begin treat Egun people well, trust go come back."

"Then the government will need to be fast in restoring trust in our land before these young men will kill you," Philip replied, and they all laughed it off.

Suddenly, Francis jumped up. He had been bitten in his right foot by a scorpion. It dug its sting into his flesh and the pain was sharp. It traveled through his nerves and escaped from his mouth. He screamed so loudly that Johnson stood briskly from his bench

and held him by the arm. Johnson sighted the grown and muscular creature, drew the machete and cut it into segments before
turning to hold Francis by the leg. Philip looked lost as to what to
do and just kept screaming, *JESUS, JESUS!* Johnson immediately
untied the cloth he had earlier knotted around the head of the
machete. He tore it into slim but lengthier piece and tied it tightly
just under Francis's right knee. As he wrapped the cloth around
the knee, Francis gnashed his teeth against his lower lips and
sweated a flood. After Johnson had carefully knotted the ends of
the cloth, he asked Philip to hold Francis because he was shaking.
He untied the boat from its anchor, quickly started the engine,
paddled their way out of the creek, and sped the boat back
towards the village.

Johnson was yelling many words, asking for help from God,
his ancestors and humans alive, while Philip kept urging Francis
to remain strong. Philip lied to Francis, whose eyelids had almost
dropped and who showed very little sign that air entered his nostrils, that they were almost at the shores of Povita where Johnson
said it would be easy to catch a vehicle to rush Francis to the hospital. Philip lied because anytime he lied, Francis would let out a
cough and his eyes would blink. And so, he told more lies. Johnson,
standing at the end of the boat, held on to the paddle as if there
was a way he could add to the speed with the long wooden stick.
And soon, there was silence as they neared the shores of Povita.

Johnson met a red wagon at his site, as he rushed out of the
boat and into Povita. It belonged to a dark and tall man with Egun
tribal marks on his cheeks who had just returned to Povita with
some passengers that were natives of Badagry. Johnson had spoken little words, but meaningless and without breath, before the

driver ran down to the banks. Philip held the kola tree to stop the boat from sailing off again, while the driver lowered and lifted Francis out of the boat. Everything happened so fast. Everybody who came to the site to help with the reconstruction of Johnson's *Badagry House* were either running after the wagon as they left for the clinic, or standing in different cells, trying to find out what had happened to Johnson and the boys he left with. There was the cell that circled around Philip as he tried to catch some air before letting out his first words of the events of that morning. And there was also the cell that seemed agitated and was already grumbling and mumbling words that meant that strangers were no more welcomed in the land. The men hung their tee-shirts around their necks and lifted the shoulders, and their chests inflated like baboons that were already fed up with poachers. The women tied their scarfs around their waists and comple-mented the yelling of their men. While all the people gathered at Johnson's reconstruction site, the red wagon faded away into a mirage, with Johnson and Francis in it.

"The people are returning in huge numbers," the driver said to Johnson. Johnson caught his stares in the rearview mir-ror as he rested Francis's head on his thigh.

"What people?" Johnson asked.

"Our people in Otodo Gbame are all returning to Badagry."

"Why that?" Johnson asked. "What will become of the waterfront?"

"The governor has asked them to leave Otodo Gbame," the driver continued. "And he has destroyed homes and thrown away our properties. They have murdered our young men. Our people are homeless in Lagos. The city doesn't want them anymore. The city doesn't want them to fish in their waters. Our people are home to take their land and their water."

THE THINGS WE PRAY FOR

Ibeji priced my body so low the day he walked up to me while I stood like a sheep without a shepherd in the dark street of Allen Avenue. His tone did not quiver when he said, *"Three Thousand Naira, last"*. He was as intimidating as the stillness that paraded the street that late hour, when all the other girls had either found their customers or gone back to the brothels because we all feared the frolics of the police who would jet into Allen Avenue and make random arrests, threaten and have sex with the girls at different dark corners dotted along the long avenue. I was, at least, determined to make my day's room rent. So, while Ibeji sauntered to my spot, staggering like he had deposited rum into his brain, I did not think of any other thing but my room's rent.

Although Ibeji oozed of a stench of gin and had sleepy and reddish eyes, I still could perceive his body cologne which smelt same as the rich people's. The fruity smell of his perfume, his fine haircut, the fairness of his skin like the emergence of the day's first sun, and his polished English were all I needed to think of a lovely night with my new client; on a night when hope seemed far-fetched and doom was bound to show in my face by dawn. *This night is for me and Ibeji.* That was all I could think of after he politely introduced himself, and also said something about photography and how my figure was fit for the lenses. I felt a quake of laughter rise from my chest, but I gave it off as a smile.

"Ruth," I said to him. And that was the first time I revealed my true name to a customer and the entire Allen Avenue.

"Feel free, Ruth," Ibeji said as we got to his hotel room and he jammed the door and turned the locks. "You can keep your handbag on the table where you can find it easily. I am aware that women and their handbags are comrades."

He let out a loud laugh. It was too loud that I knew it wasn't my navy blue fake Gucci handbag that made him giggle. I knew it wasn't me too. I knew it was not what I could see or imagine. It was rather the feeling of accomplishment that only a full dose of alcohol could give. Alcohol makes us laugh, and cry, and scream. Eve, my roommate, once said that alcohol brings out the truth from our lips, after a group of girls at the brothel had so much beer that they fought till early dawn and kept throwing abusive words. All the other tenants just stood and watched without saying a word, until the skinny girl said something about how the chubby and dark-skinned girl had infected plenty Ikeja men with STDs. As soon as her words were let out into the little courtyard of the brothel, it echoed from room to room and woke those that slept. More girls gathered around the courtyard. Some laughed at what she said, some placed their hands on their heads, while some cheered the warring girls even more. That was when the chubby girl ran into her room and never came out that night. But her last words were, "You that have AIDS *nkor?*"

"They have exposed themselves, Rita," Eve said to me as we returned to the room to recount our dealings of the day. "Look at what alcohol makes you do. They just exposed their secrets."

I wanted to tell Eve that my name was not Rita. But she had been calling me Rita for over eleven months, and the name had stuck to her lips because she was fond of me. *Rita, I love your shape.*

Rita, I love your wig. Rita, see how much I made from one mugu last night. Rita, I have gathered enough money to help maale pay for her shop. Popsy will never accept any gift or cash from me, Rita. Rita, I am the black sheep of my house. So I couldn't tell her that night. And just like the other many times, I promised myself I was going to let her know the truth the next day.

But there I was, in a hotel room with a stranger who I had already told my real name, drinking from a glass of wine he had poured before walking into the bathroom, hammering the door loudly against the frame.

"I can't find where to keep my bag on your table," I screamed as I heard the shower and his attempt to sing Bob Marley's One Love. "You have your camera, lenses, and laptop all over. I wouldn't wish to damage any of these expensive things, *biko*. I'll simply drop my bag on the floor."

Ibeji giggled loudly, and it echoed. He said something that I didn't hear. Then he stopped.

My eyes caught a few photographs on the desk. They were photographs of beautiful women; black women, scarcely clad and sexy. One of these ladies, a young girl that looked like she was in her twenties, wore panties and only covered her breasts with her arms. It was such fine photography and the colors said something about the photographer's know-how. They were all different women and Ibeji had left their photos on the desk with his camera and lenses. Ibeji was a photographer. He had earlier told me, but I wasn't quite listening. The amount of money he priced me for the night beclouded my reasoning. And even though I really wanted to follow him, I also needed him to understand the sort of pleasure he was about to experience as I had a reputation for leaving my customers satisfied and asking for more sex. So I hatched a plan about how I would kneel down and have his rod in my mouth, and have him name a better price before letting him feel the hot and wet inside of me.

Ibeji did not allow any of my plans to hatch. He emerged from the bathroom with a white towel tied around his loins, slumped into the bed and rested his head on the white pillow. Water from his head ran down and rested on the pillowcase, and wet marks widened as more water dropped. Ibeji began to snore as I contemplated starting up the conversation about my fees. He slept like a new infant, and sometimes his snores would break into sequences as though one attempted too much to start a generator without oil. I gave up on my plan, as I stood and unzipped my flowery gown and let it drop on the tiled floor. I lifted my legs and walked into the bathroom where steams from Ibeji's bath had already fogged the mirror. I felt the heat from his bath, but I did not let the thought of the temperature bother me. I turned the knobs of the hot and cold water faucet, and let the water rain on my palms to get a perfect warm mix. And when I was happy with the temperature, I stood on the bath tray and let the water wash down from my face to my breasts, and along the lines of my cleavage.

* * * * *

"Hey, baby," Ibeji whispered into my ears. His words sounded like the echoes of my dream, soothing and reassuring. But it was long I had such a pleasing dream in which a voice spoke so calmly to me. Usually, one hardly dream at the brothel. It was not a place to sleep and dream of anything. We hardly slept. And when we finally slept, we hardly dreamt for the very few hours we could afford to shut our eyes. The few times I dreamt while asleep at the brothel, they were not dreams. They were my fears. They were about Mama Bisola dancing about the courtyard, asking for money for the food I ate at her *buka*. They were about Alhaji, our landlord, clapping for Mama Bisola, and encouraging her to drag me out of my room and beat me up. It wasn't really a dream, except that those thoughts happened while I fell asleep. Dreams like that were things that happened in reality because the landlord was a wicked and shameless man with conspicuous tribal marks. He fanned all the troubles and fights between tenants and whoever they owed. For all of us at the brothel, dreams were not about fairies and flowers and wonderlands, or many beautiful things. For all of us, dreams were only a continuation of the horror we lived in. So when I heard Ibeji's voice that morning, my eyes freely opened and I saw his beautiful demeanor looking down at me with a smile.

"Good morning, Ibeji."

"Good morning, dear," Ibeji whispered. "I can't ask you how your night was. I've been sitting here for over an hour, watching you sleep like an angel."

"Oh, that's quite romantic," I said. I felt moisture erupt around my womanhood. "You must be quite a gentleman."

"No, I'm not," he replied. "I'm only a hungry man in need of lovemaking with an angel with the best body in the world."

And Ibeji lowered his face to meet mine. We kissed. It was not lips touching lips. It was a real kiss as our tongues found each other and sucked away in the heat of passion. It was not long before Ibeji kissed my face, my neck, my breasts, and my tummy.

97

I pulled his face back up, he raised my gown, and I felt him slide into my wetness. My mouth could not hold back the passion. I cannot remember how loud I yelled for a rescue I knew that I never needed, or how many times I used the words "Make love to me, baby". The feeling was quite what I needed that morning. All the sweats that dropped from his neck and married my already soaked breasts, the moans that we could not hush, the name callings, and the clenching and nail scars all came together as our honest desire to have each other. We did not remember that we had made love without condoms, although I saw them on the stool after Ibeji had erupted and slumped on me.

We lay side by side, gazing aloft at the ceiling, while Ibeji panted like he had just won an Olympic race. It was then I noticed I had been undressed, and my gown was lifeless on the tiled floor. Ibeji did not say so much for the many minutes we lay in bed, holding each other's hands and taking in all the air in the air-conditioned room. It wasn't after many minutes that he coughed and said something about the water heater not working that morning because the electricity in the hotel was powered by a low capacity generator. He also said that he had insisted that the air conditioner be left working, even against the hotel's regulations for using the air conditioners with generators. And then Ibeji brought out a bundle of cash from the side drawer of the table that had all the unused condoms on it. He dropped it on my chest, stood up and walked into the bathroom to wash off the sweat and fluids of sex.

"I know we agreed on something less," Ibeji said to me, holding my arms. We had both showered and cleaned up together. He had said that was what lovers did—bathe together.

"We agreed on three thousand naira."

"I know."

"This is twenty kay here, Ibeji."

"I know," he replied. "And it is not for the sex we had, Ruth. Look at us. Just look at us. Aren't we more than a one night stand? Are we not going to see again to do even more than we just did? To love each other even more, and take your beauty to places you never imagined? Aren't we going to make more than you have in your hands?"

"I don't get you, Ibeji," I said.

"You don't get me?"

"No. Yes. I mean, how are we going to make more than this together?"

Ibeji brought out his business card from his breast pocket and placed in my hand, the hand that held the cash. He then folded my fingers into a fist and urged me to call him later in the day. He said I was to visit his office well dressed. He said he would change my life and make me his own for as long as I was willing. I was willing and I desired Ibeji, as much as he wanted me. And so with smiles and warm feelings, I nodded to every word he said.

* * * * *

Four months after we first made love, Ibeji told me everything about making me his top model and property. It was a few weeks after I had made my first money from modeling for corporate brands and showing up on portraits at Ibeji's exhibition, with a couple of calls demanding that I play a movie role. It was a few days after I had realized that my life had changed, and the way I dressed, the pubs I visited, the friends I had newly made and the new men that wooed me, that I left my luggage with Eve and moved in with Ibeji into his Lekki apartment. As soon as I stepped into his beautiful living room, the day of my final decision, he planted a kiss on my forehead. He forced my mobile phone out of my hands, opened the back and took out the sim card.

"You won't need this mobile number anymore," Ibeji said. "It belongs to Allen. I got you a new number that belongs to the Island. Now you have a new life. Let the old go."

I loved the new life, although it was full of hard work, meetings, learning and the late nights that I was already used to. I loved living with Ibeji. I enjoyed all the feelings I got from the attention he gave and the way he made sure to introduce me to all his friends and associates, and never forgot to say that I was his girlfriend. I loved the joy that glittered all over him and how he sweated trying to make his staff tidy up the studio, get my make-up done and choose my costumes anytime we were shooting for a magazine or a campaign. I was his new joy. I was the only thing he missed in his life after running back from Amsterdam, leaving behind his two-year-old marriage to a Caucasian who was a few years older than he was and who made life in the Netherlands miserable for him. I was his new poetry, his photography and his art. Ibeji knew everyone around him knew he had found happiness, but he said he didn't care about any other thing in the world.

While I took a little walk around the living room that had just become mine, I touched every figurine as though in response to their greetings and ran my fingers on the long leather sofa as a pianist would run his fingers on all the keys of the piano. The air smelt differently—of almond, of lemon tea and coffee, of cigarettes smoked days before, of Asian spices, of loneliness. The loneliness had come to an end, the loneliness that would never allow me to return to Allen Avenue, and to Eve and all her fondness towards me.

It was then I remembered I had left Eve without a word. I had left her without a revelation of who I was, and all the real stories, that I was not from Ilesha, that I was Egun and ran away from Makoko to fend for myself. I remembered I had left her with a lot of lies, things she would never find out about me, things that would remain a burden to my heart. Against Ibeji's instructions, I was going to search for Eve's mobile number. I was going to quickly call her and tell her I had moved on, and she could visit anytime. I was going to tell her all the things I kept secret, apologize to her and cajole her into finding an eligible boyfriend for her, one of Ibeji's friends.

"Rita, is that you?" Eve said.

"Yes, Eve," I replied. "It's me o!"

"Bad girl," she said. She let out a very loud giggle.

"What?"

"So you're Ruth. That's your real name. Your photographs are everywhere. Rita, oh sorry, Ruth, whatever, you've made it. You're now a big Island girl oh."

"You found out?" I said. The words were too heavy on my lips. "Many times, I wanted to let you know this. Many times, I stuttered. We were in the streets, Eve. Our lives were already messed up."

"What are you saying, Rita?" Eve said. "You're not making any sense."

"I'm sorry."

"It's all right. My roomie is now a celebrity. I'm happy. Are you coming back to this place?"

"No, Eve. Ibeji has asked that I stay with him in Lekki. It's beautiful here."

"Good. Don't come back to this place. This place is not for humans. We are all dogs and pigs here. No one is even sure of tomorrow. Stay on the Island and enjoy life with your boyfriend."

"Thank you, Eve. I was lucky to have met someone as good-hearted as you. You are such an angel, Eve."

Those were the few words I could say before I choked on my saliva and teardrops began to run down my cheeks. For the first time, I knew I had lost the freedom of my poverty. I had lost my ability to walk down to Mama Bisola's buka, with men hissing at me and calling me *fine gehl*. I had lost my free ticket to view the many fights that happened between the girls; the *okada* riders who staggered into the brothel, drunk, and asking to have sex with us; the landlord who cursed the girls that locked their doors on the days he came to collect rent; and the many dramas that happened in the night. I had just lost Eve.

"Hello," Eve said. "Hello. Are you still there?"

"Yes, Eve" I replied.

"It's not Eve oh. My name is not Evelyn. And I'm not from Delta State."

"You mean?"

"My real name is Chekwube. I am from Awka in Anambra State."

THE THINGS WE LOVE

When she opened her mouth to speak, she sounded like Michelle Obama. I told her this many times to make her feel noble, but she insisted that I was selfish and gave her no form of attention. She wanted me to treat her the same way I treated my ID card which I hung forever around my neck every week. She knew I always hung my ID around my neck each morning before I left for work. After work, I dropped it on the keyboard of the blue laptop, together with the car key and business cards. And some nights, she would catch me sneaking to the reading desk to confirm if it was still there, safe, and in one piece. Then she would mumble some words of unhappiness that sent heat along my spine, even as I would never get to know what she was trying to say. But she knew it was not the ID that I loved so much. She knew it was my job at the multinational firm, but she insisted that I treated her the same way I treated the plastic card with the inscription "TOTAL" on it. Who would fiddle with a nagging girlfriend? Who would take a scorpion along with him wherever he went? Who would hang Lola around his neck? Who would treat Lola like a TOTAL job?

"Honorable is coming to town," Ricky said. He lifted his glass of wine and sipped some of the Sauvignon Blanc before squinting his eyes as though it stung his cheeks. "He wants to host us to a dinner and some clubbing."

"That's wonderful," I said. "I better start looking for better lies to tell Lola. She can be a witch. That girl!"

Ricky laughed audibly. I felt the eyes of the other merrymakers at the dance lounge peer into me.

"I have two Uniport girls o!" Ricky announced, throwing fists in the air of the pub like one rehearsing a boxing match. "Instagram cannot fail me, Tamunosa. I told you to join me. You refused."

"You mean am?" I asked, trying to sound excited. I tried to sound excited because that was what Ricky expected of me. That was how he would have responded if I was the one who came with the breaking news that I had found new *nyash*. That was how every guy-man in Port Harcourt responded whenever such news of a possible escapade came. It was a cliché of a response, anyway. But it always fired up such mischievous conversations.

"Better look for what to tell that your girlfriend o. No one is going home that night. We are all getting wasted and ending up at Charade Hotel. I'm getting that part sorted also."

"When is it again?"

"When is what?"

"When is Honorable coming to town? Does he not have a date yet?"

"Oh, that?" Ricky said. "In a fortnight. Just leave your weekend blank, no other engagements. We can't afford not to be complete for this groove, man."

Ricky continued talking about many other things, from business to office issues, and religion. Ricky was not a believer in anything. He laughed at the sight of televangelists, and mocked you anytime you mentioned you went to church. He said it was all a waste of one's life, except that life itself is way too boring and needed such activities to distract man and keep him engaged. Ricky believed in so many awkward things, and his wittiness made you almost let go of your faith in the God you had been taught to believe in from the day of your birth. Whenever Ricky came with those assertions, I quickly shoved them off with another topic.

Ricky was my smart colleague, the one whom my line manager trusted for all presentations on behalf of the department. The way he spoke, how he gestured and the beauty of his PowerPoint presentations won him the heart of many meetings, in and out of the country. Ricky hardly dressed to make a statement, not like some of us who spent a few more hours in the mirror because Lola wouldn't let you leave the house without an erect shirt collar, ironed trousers and shiny leather belts that usually matched the shoes in color. Ricky was simple, but not with women. He was the famous guy in the University of Port Harcourt and the talk of Rivers State University of Science and Technology. How he managed to get into the good books of these uni girls is still a wonder to us, his friends. But Ricky was not a bad company. At least, the scents of his promiscuous lifestyle and the crumbs of his attempts got to us in many ways. When Ricky needed to call a girl to join us at Metro Lounge, he counted how many boys we were at our corner and then he asked his girl to come over with the same number of pretty university girls, so we could all be treated just as fine as he.

A fortnight after Ricky had first told me about Honorable's coming to town, I had already bought Lola's heart with a new iPhone 8plus and many trips to different restaurants, from Chinese to Igbo and Yoruba specialized chefs. And after all these trips and intense sensual satisfactions, Lola still made me promise I was going to return home immediately after our meeting with Honorable. For her, sleeping in hotels was a waste of money and an invitation to a conclave of infidelity. She kept sounding her guns of warning, telling me how Port Harcourt girls have been found to be promiscuous with sexually transmitted ailments. Finally, I succumbed to Lola and her pleas and made her all the promises as she forced them out of my mouth. I knew I was not going to keep those promises, but I loved to believe I would.

At Metro Lounge where we had agreed to receive Honorable, we sat with three girls from the state university. The loud music that played in the early hours of the evening deafened my ears and saved me from the many words I wanted to say to Ibitamuno, although she seemed as though she didn't need so much of an *aristo's* lies before she would accept that of three of the girls, she was the one who stole my gaze for the evening. Ibitamuno was an engineering student at the state university, and she was in her finals. It was easy to discuss structures with her, and all aspects of reinforcements in construction. She had this small voice that gave her off as an infant, but she was firm and sure with her voice, which made her arguments on why the government and private sectors should be encouraged to collaborate to give birth to projects that follow required specifications. Ibitamuno had not only caught my attention because of her brilliance and rare beauty but also because she was a Bonny Island girl. Coming from my part of the world, it was a delight to listen to her as she gestured and demonstrated everything she said, and her voice kept sinking deep into oblivion by the ascension of the Afro-pop music played at Metro Lounge. I nodded a few more times, even though I had stopped hearing her. And then, she stopped. It wasn't long before everyone started nodding or dancing to the music played that she threw the plea eye at me. We would soon be on the dance floor, showing off how best we swayed new dance moves.

"I'm not sure he'll be able to make it to this place," Ricky screamed into my ears. He had ordered another bottle of Sauvignon Blanc and shoved a glass of it to my face. He then took my right hand and wrapped my fingers around the tall glass.

"Not a call from him. I've called him several times, but I haven't been able to get across."

"It's all right, Ricky," I said, trying to suppress the loudness and chattering around.

Ibitamuno turned and bent forward, lowering her bum, she rocked it against my loins and I felt a quick rush of blood down my veins. My loins hardened against her bum, and she turned and smiled at me. I held her by the waist and rocked in rhythm to her movements.

"Oh boy, you be fool o!" Ricky yelled at me. And then, he chuckled. "I dey here dey talk about Honorable, you dey grab waist. Keep grabbing waist."

"Wetin man go do?" I replied. "What do you want me to do, with this kind of soft something before me? I didn't kill Christ. Remember."

Ricky laughed so loudly that we joined him. The two other girls showed up and held Ricky from his front and back, and danced against his body, forcing him to move according to the sound of the music. Ibitamuno turned and faced me, and stamped a kiss on my lips. It felt so right, her lips on mine. It felt soft, like the kiss of a university girl, like the kiss of a much younger female. I felt the random rush of blood all through my veins. I felt like I was new, like I was also a university lad, with sagged and shredded denim jeans and a *wanna-wanna* accent to have wooed one of the prettiest girls I had seen. But then, I remembered I wore my straight cut American IZOD jeans which I bought on my last trip to Maryland, with a well-starched and tucked in Calvin Klein shirt that revealed a shiny Gucci leather belt. I was not a university lad that was obligated to no one. I was what university girls called Aristo, a married womanizer who swooned at the sight of pretty young girls.

There was a gunshot inside Metro Lounge. It was so loud that it doused the loud music into complete silence. And then there were more shots and more before silence reigned over the space like the sound of a graveyard in the middle of the night. Someone screamed aloud. She was a girl, but I did not see her face. The only thing visible in the entire hall was the multi-colored disco light that danced about from floor to ceiling. There was another gunshot which gave off like a race starter, and clubbers who were at the entrance rose and scurried towards our corner in search of floor spaces to prostrate. Ibitamuno clenched my arms tightly, and for the first time, I noticed she had been by my side ever since. The scent of her hair gave off her identity, as the disco light was not enough to see her face.

"Jesus," Ibitamuno whispered. "Blood of Jesus. Blood of Jesus."

"Say no more," I hushed her. "You have to keep your cool."

Ibitamuno went mute at once. But the clench of her fingers grew tighter and quaked around my arms. It was the quake of fear. It was a quake not uncommon with Nigerian women. Ibitamuno was not any different from most Nigerian women who were lavish with the use of the blood of Jesus. They used his blood at the sight of any danger, danger as little as the presence of a cockroach or mice. Every woman sprayed the blood of Jesus in airplanes to clear the air of any crash, or on interstate major roads for the fear of vehicle collisions that could be fatal. Every morning, in Nigerian homes and churches, the blood of Jesus is invoked to clear the path for the day. And all business owners used it to launch the day. If the blood of Jesus was rationed from country to country, Nigerians would have been borrowing from other countries. It was also not scarce on Lola's lips, as she moaned it in whispers during passionate sex without a single thought of what the implications of using the blood of the son of God during sex could result to. Lola would have definitely been shaken, even more than Ibitamuno, if she had been the one with me that night at the Metro Lounge.

"Where is Honorable Tami Johnson?" one of the gunmen bellowed. He sounded like the leader of the gang. His voiced rocked every corner of the space, and the fear it created moved a few more people. Our bodies rubbed off against each other.

"Where is Honorable? We know you are here. Don't waste much of our time. If we pick you out by ourselves, we will surely blow your brains off."

"Honorable, you no dey hear?" another one yelled. "Abi you wan make we begin shoot everybody before you comot? You want everyone to die before you come out?"

Someone from our corner said something, and the men asked him to stand up. He stood up and spoke in low tones to them. And although his voice was low, it was not so hard for me to figure out the information he made available to the gunmen. He was the manager of the dance lounge. He had been informed of

Honorable's visit to the club and had come around to be able to receive him. But he had not seen Honorable at the lounge that time of the night. Honorable was yet to be at the lounge.

"Maybe you guys came too early," he said. And we heard a loud clap sound which seemed like a slap. The manager fell to the floor, and I felt it was not that serious until someone screamed, 'Blood!' Then voices started rising from all corners. People were beginning to yell and cry out to the gang for mercy as the manager had already confirmed the absence of the member of the Federal House of Representatives at the lounge.

"Shut up, all of you!" he yelled. "Just keep quiet! A few minutes ago you were here drinking, dancing and pressing *nyash*. Now you are calling on God's name. Just shut up. God is not as sinful as you. He will not hear you. We will kill all of you. No time. Produce this man we are looking for. We know he is here."

"But he's not here," someone said. The voice rose from near our corner. There was something familiar about the voice. "He never came here. I'm sure of that."

"Hey, Oga who you be?" the gang leader asked. "Who are you? And how do you know?"

"My name is Patrick Osa."

My eyes forced open. *No, Ricky. Don't do this. Don't tell him you know the Honorable and that we have been waiting for him. Don't tell him anything about us. Please, Ricky, please.* I said all that in my head. I could not utter a word, as it seemed like my heart pumped faster and my body had begun to tremble.

"Where is Honorable?" asked the gang leader.

"I don't know, sir," Ricky said, his voice quivering as he spoke. "I have called him a couple of times. He never took my calls. He is not here. Please, don't cause anyone injury. We don't know anything about what is going on here."

"Oh, you know him. He's your friend."

"No. I have only met him a couple of times. I cannot defend his personality with great faith."

"Oyinbo! You are speaking grammar," the gunman said. "Arabi!"

"Oga, I dey here," the third member of the gang walked in from the exit. "What am I doing for you?"

"Show this one something," the gang leader uttered. "Clear em doubt! He thinks it's by using the most expensive perfume. Every man has a bad odor. Bring out the odor in him. He's leaving with us."

For the remaining part of the dark night, we heard Ricky crying for help from the hall and his voice evaporated towards the exit. We heard him yell and cry that whatever they did to him hurt so badly and he didn't deserve all the persecution served him. Ricky's voice grew stronger as he cried in defense. But the stronger it grew, the louder and harder the beatings rained on him. And after a few more minutes, his cries faded with the bellows of the criminal gang.

"Make we jazz out!" yelled the gang leader. "Let us leave before someone calls SARS police on us."

They left as soon as those words left his mouth. They left behind a silence which lasted for a couple of minutes. And as we all stood to check ourselves and straighten our bodies, quietness was still kept. As the lights went on, I saw Ibitamuno squatting on the floor, completely traumatized; she shook like she had been thrown out in the snow without a jacket. I stooped by her side and held her to steady her body, but it shook ceaselessly and her teeth gnashed aloud. The manager walked up to us as we sat on the floor. He was badly injured on the forehead and still bled. But he was able to move around a little bit more to ensure everyone was safe. It was a dark night. It was a night of fear, of silence, of many things we never prayed to happen that would change our lives.

* * * * *

Three years after the night at Metro Lounge, Lola pushed me aside to make way for her to exit the house as she dragged her last luggage with her. She had earlier sent out most of her things. She was fed up with our relationship and had rented a new place in the GRA.

"Get out, Tamunosa," she screamed. "Get out of my way. You are completely useless. You destroyed the joy in me. You killed everything. Now, what is my gain?"

Lola said I did not give her happiness, and that she was ready to set off on the road to finding it by herself. I did not tell her that our constant brawl was becoming even more boring. I did not tell her that I had found new love in Ibitamuno and that she would soon return from Abuja after her national service, and that we had agreed on trying to work things out. I did not tell Lola that I had promised that she would be gone by the time Ibitamuno would be ready to return and that she was to return in two months. I never let Lola know that her selfishness had blinded her from my grief and pains of not being able to find Ricky or know his whereabouts since after the night at Metro Bar. As I stood and watched her jam the exit gate and left, I felt for the first time in three years, the smiles and hope of a new beginning, a light of hope.

THE THINGS WE BECOME

Nwamma had asked me a lot of times before that Monday morning to bring my penis out from the zipper. She called it *pee-pee*, and sometimes she called it *nta-nta*, like it was one of those succulent animal skins mom served as *nkwobi* to Dad's special guests on Sundays. She would grab it in her hands and rub it until it stiffens, and she would ask me to zip it back inside my trousers. Nwamma said it was not yet ready for use, but was already as fine and smooth as the buttocks of an infant; a brand new baby that had just been carried out of the labor room. They made me smile; the things Nwamma said to me about my penis, my lips and my nipples that were beginning to sprout like little thorns off the trunk of an orange tree. I loved her words so much because they came in hushed tones and whispers. She warned that I was not to tell mom or Sister Ngo all she said and did to me. She was going to stop if I told them. She was never going to be friendly anymore. I needed this friendship more than any other thing that went on in the house. So I made Nwamma a promise not to tell mom or Sister Ngo all the things that happened to me.

That Monday morning, as we went on mid-term break and stayed away from school for a whole week, Nwamma held my penis in her hands, rubbed it a few more times than before and it became stiffer than it had ever been. While I lay on her mat, she pulled off her underwear and threw it on the cement floor, she sat on my loins and rocked and moaned in many words I could not unravel. Although I did not understand why Nwamma panted and moaned those words, and smiled when she eventually stopped and slumped by my side, I was glad I made her smile as a reward for all the soothing words she said to me that made me feel like a grown man. *You're a man,* she would keep telling me in the many weeks to come, and it did not matter to me that I was nine years old. All that mattered was that assurance; that confirmation from mom's pretty maid that I had become old enough to eat food cooked for the elderly.

* * * * *

"Honey, I made it!" Urenna screamed from the staircase. It did not matter that we lived on the second floor of the six-flat apartment building; the echoes of her voice bellowed all the way up from the ground floor. The sound of her sweet voice jostled me up from the recliner and quickened my feet down the risers of the stairs.

"Really?" I said to her as we met midway. I held her in my embrace and kept whispering my doubts in her ears.

"Yes, I'm sure," she replied. "I got the job at the airline as Customer Care Assistant. The manager says it's just a starter. He promises a quick promotion. He said there are senior level gaps to fill."

"Oh wow, sweetie," I said and loosened my grip on her arms. "This is some good news. I'm even speechless."

"I told you I was *gonna* get this particular one. I told you."

We both giggled. Urenna vibrated all over as she laughed. It had been long I last saw her let out that sort of air in her. We stood on the landing of the stairs, held both hands together, and while her handbag dropped without care on the floor, we giggled ceaselessly like we had inhaled some fair volume of Nitrous Oxide.

For the many times that Urenna laughed and shook her body in rhythm of the glee, I feared she would lose the two months fetus in her womb. And I would hug and steady her, the same way I held her in my embrace until she stopped giggling the day she brought the news of her new job. But for the many days after she started taking too many calls from friends and family that needed to learn a thing or two about flight schedules, Urenna grumbled more than she laughed, or she would simply put up with the *it-is-well* smile that spelled disbelief all over her face.

As she approached the later months of her pregnancy and the doctor let us know that it was a baby boy and that it was why he kicked the walls of the womb so much and punched his fists through Urenna's tummy, the new job became even more of a sad news than good. She would hardly get out of bed in the mornings without complaining of a backache and how unreasonable I was for not feeling her pains.

Mom said it was the pregnancy that made Urenna nag and rant gibberish all the time. Urenna said she was not ranting and that her words were not gibberish. But mom assured her she would become better and brighter after the birth of our son. Mom made sure to send Urenna all the awkward things and food she asked for, from *nzu* to *udara*. She would ask her younger sister, Sister Ngo, who was still unmarried, to help her send them across to Urenna. Once, mom called me and asked why I had not yet returned from work.

"I work late, mom," I replied.

"Don't you know you have a pregnant wife at home? Tell your boss if he doesn't know. You must be home early."

"But everything is fine, mom."

"Everything is not fine, Ikenna," mom said. She sounded aggravated by my answers.

They were obviously the wrong choice of words. "Urenna keeps calling. She needs all the love and care. I'm sure that's all she needs. She keeps asking for rare things."

"Mom, that is Urenna for you," I said. "She keeps acting up, especially since you announced that she is at liberty to boss everyone around."

"No. Don't say that," Mom replied. "She just called now. She said she needs to smell an armpit. How weird that could be. I've never heard or seen that.

"Shebi I told you, mom. Thank God you can now see for yourself."

"Anyway, I told her to wait for you to return. She wouldn't smell my old grey-haired armpit; you know that quite well, Ikenna."

"But she said that? That she needs to smell someone's armpit? That sounds stupid."

"Sadly, it is not stupid. It is what we women go through for you men. So you better rush home with that your armpit and let your wife sniff them. Silly boy. Nothing is to happen to my grandson. I already named him Akubueze. And that is what you will call him. Ekwuchagom!"

Mom hung the call. It was the first time throughout that day that I had to feel pearls of sweat trickle and run down my cheeks from my head. It was the first time in the many months of Urenna's pregnancy that fears stuffed my chest, leaving me with very little space for air. I raised my right hand to my tie knot and loosened my red tie. It was a Friday but I had worn a tie to the firm because we had booked series of clients' briefing meetings throughout the day, and I had prepared a lot of presentation drawings for our elitist clients. My job as the Project Architect of Cube Consult meant I represented the entire design and construction team before our clients who were usually the wealthy bunch of Lagos Island. There was the pretty Barrister Titi Horsefall, the single and evenly bleached lady in her midlife. There was the sexual myth everyone at the firm believed and made jokes about, about her advances towards me. After Urenna expressed her fears for the powerful society lady's special fondness of me, I began to notice it was not mere fondness.

Titi had called earlier to inform me that she wouldn't make it to the meeting at the firm. She would meet the governor earlier in the day and then visit her property agents later on. She would also be catching up with a few of her partners and the Ladies of Lagos Island. She asked if we could reschedule. But when I fumbled with my response, she offered to host me to a dinner at Eko Premier Hotel, which was five-star and asked me if I preferred Chinese to European continental dishes. Titi was not going to let me think about accepting her invitation. She had immediately sent her assistant out to make the required reservations.

"7 p.m, Ike," she announced. "Tunde has booked for 7 p.m."

"Okay, ma," I replied. "I'll be there."

As Titi ended the call, the fears of sitting face-to-face on a table-for-two with a high-class Lagos Island lady in a five-star restaurant filled my stomach. It was some sort of happiness mixed with uncertainties. It was the fear of what to say if Titi wanted to talk about vain things that gripped me even more. So,

I quickly printed out all the layout and 3D drawings, and I arranged them as a portfolio. I was going to shove it in her face the moment we meet and she would have no reason to talk about things that were quite unrelated.

"Come on, Ike," Titi said. She waved her hands in disapproval as we stood in the large hotel lobby and waited for the chauffeur to lead us to the restaurant.

"You can let Tunde have all the drawings. He'll take them to the car. I asked for a dinner date, not another boring business meeting after a hectic day in Lagos."

"Yes, Architect," Tunde said and gestured. "Let me have them. Hakeem would be driving me back home. We would have to keep them for madam at the house."

"Your driver is leaving?" I asked, hardly staring into Titi's eyes.

"Yes, he's leaving," Titi replied. "And it was rude of me not to have asked you for a lift home after the dinner. Hakeem needs to run some errands at once."

"That's not a problem," I said. "It's nothing I cannot do for my biggest client."

"And friend, Tunde."

"Yes, ma'am. And friend too."

When we got to our table, it was just the two of us. Titi gleamed in a flowing red gown with shiny sequence dotted all over, and her body spoke like she was in her twenties, slim and sexy enough to send seductive thoughts into the head of any admirer. And for a moment, since I met Titi for the first time as she walked into the firm asking for the Project Architect, I felt I owned her. I moved Titi's chair for her to sit comfortably before I sat in mine.

"Lagos is a crazy place. A lot of people chasing this money. No one really cares about the next person," Titi said.

We had filled our glasses with sweet red wine, selected our entrée from the menu, with Chris Deburgh's Lady in Red playing through speakers fixed in ceiling vents and hanging on the walls. Eko Premier Hotel's Queen of Sheba Restaurant smelt of different spices and Arabian perfumes and Titi said they were Ethiopian spices. She said Ethiopians were the best cooks and she was sure I was going to enjoy my meals. And although I did not know what Ethiopians food tasted like, I was willing to explore because Titi glowed even more beautiful as she tried to persuade me. Titi had this charm that made you say YES when you meant to say NO. Titi could easily make you hide your face, as looking into her eyes had this feeling of defeat and helplessness it brought to you. Titi was magical, and it was not long before I started to desire to have her as mine.

But with Titi, you still felt the sting of fear, of uncertainty—if she would walk you out of the restaurant for trying to tell her how beautiful she was and how she made your bladder fill up with hot liquid anytime you stole a glance of the magic in her eyes. As fair as winter, with a voice that warmed your heart like a sauna, you knew you could not hold those words in your head for too long before they would burst out before both of you. And while you were fighting with your demons, Titi stretched her arm and held your hand to the table.

"It's all right, Ike," Titi said to me. "Feel comfortable with me. Our friendship has nothing to do with my business with your firm. I already told you that."

119

"Yes, Titi," I replied. I raised my face to her, and for a moment my eyes did not flicker as we ogled each other in the face. I felt some sense of oneness with Titi, like she was my prized possession. That was what Titi wanted from me. That was why she smiled and heaved as I called her by her name.

"You know I'm fond of you, Ike," she said, breaking the silence of my thoughts. "We can be there for each other and no one would even know. I'm sure you know what I mean, Ike."

I wanted to say yes to her, but I was not sure that would be a good start. I wasn't sure I needed this rendezvous with Titi. I was young in Lagos, with a pregnant wife, and that was all every Lagos boy prayed for; to hop in bed with an influential Sisi Eko and enjoy all the free luxury that came with it. Titi did not sound like she needed a one night stand. She was fond of me, and that fondness is not something she would allow to breathe for just one night of passion and heat. Titi was older than I was. Her voice and accents were quite intimidating. She would have her way around me and have me in her vagina at every single urge.

* * * * *

Ten years after mom sent Nwamma out of the house because Sister Ngo had seen her bring out my *pee-pee* from the zipper, and because mom was beginning to grow uncomfortable about how she was always around me, we met at the supermarket by the street. Nwamma had grown into a full woman, with huge breasts and curves around her waist. It was Nwamma who first called my name and said I had grown into a big man. It was Nwamma who spread her arms and took me in a tight embrace, letting her breasts press against my chest, cushioning me into a brief pleasure. After mom and Sister Ngo sent her back to her aunt in town, she had to sell housewares at the market with her. This she did until she was able to fund her way out of secondary school. It wasn't really so easy for her outside our home. Nwamma told me everything she had gone through, as though she went through all that for me.

"I am the new receptionist at the motel down the street," she said. Her voice was soft and threw many memories at me. They were memories of my childhood, and how my innocence was stolen from me.

"That's nice, Nwamma."

"You're free to come over anytime. We do not have many customers yet. We are just starting. It is boring at the motel. I am always the only one around, except of course the gateman."

"That's all right, Nwamma. I will come over in the evening. We are on a long vacation from the university."

"Cool. I'll be delighted to have you."

At the motel, no one was around the premises, not even the security man. It was as quiet as the death of the day. The only life that existed in the premises, besides Nwamma and I, were the lizards that scurried for safety as I stood at the entrance with Nwamma. Nwamma said the security man had to rush home to have dinner, as the motel was yet to start feeding them. Nwamma did not say any other word before she dragged me into one of the rooms of the motel and planted a kiss on my lips. She then held me tightly and brought her face closer to mine. I kissed her passionately, letting my tongues dip into her mouth and connect with her tongue. I tasted her and she tasted me back. And we breathed into each other's nostrils. Nwamma unbuttoned her white work shirt and threw it to the chair by the dressing mirror, while her skirt fell from her waist and slumped on the floor beneath her. She pulled my belt and the hook left the hole, and I watched as she went down with her face on my loins, the thing she had always loved all her life. It was not long before I was on top of Nwamma, pounding my lust away. Different images of the years of my infancy played out before me like a cinema, while Nwamma moaned in the pleasure of satisfaction. And then guilt and hatred took over my spirit. Venom of bitterness stung my heart and my hunger for Nwamma shrunk like the eyes of a snail.

Nwamma began to fight and claw my hands as I held her against the bed, squeezing my clench on her neck, taking every air out of her. She kicked her legs in the air. She tried to say some words, maybe plead for life, for a second chance to right her wrongs. But I was filled with hatred against her for the many things she did to my life, for stealing my innocence and taking my smiles away with her. As Nwamma wriggled and kicked the more, I tightened my grip and pressed her even the more. And it was not long before Nwamma's eyes turned white and her body went cold. I staggered out of her body, found my clothes and dashed out of the hotel premises, with no sense of guilt in me. Even when the news of Nwamma's shameful death went round the estate, and also when Sister Ngo came to the house just to tell mom that Nwamma's dead body was found nude, I simply gathered my luggage and returned to the university.

* * * * *

"No, Titi," I said, and stood up from the table at the restaurant. "I can't do this. And I need to return to the office quickly."

"What? How?" Titi stuttered. She stood up before me. "You don't have to leave, even if you do not wish for us to happen."

"No, Titi," I repeated. "You won't understand."

"Then make me understand."

"I am leaving, ma'am. I have to finish work at the firm."

www.ingramcontent.com/pod-product-compliance
Lightning Source LLC
Chambersburg PA
CBHW030351180626
46812CB00007B/2844